PHOENIXES, DRAGONS, AND ALIENS:

ATLANTIS

A MOST PROBABLE STORY/S SERIES
"FLYING" DEEP WITHIN

---CODES---

VOLUME ONE

"BIRTHED BY FIRE"

"THE PHOENIX"

HER STORY....
your beginning..?

BY DR. R. LOWERY-HAWK

"PONDER-ENLIGHT"

Enlightening Books To Ponder Upon

ISBN–13: 978-1534882539

ISBN-1534882537

Copyright © 2016 Dr. R. Lowery-Hawk

Drawing Of Rainbow Phoenix by Dr. R. Lowery-Hawk

All rights reserved. This book or any portion thereof may not be reproduced or used in any manner whatsoever without the excess written permission of the publisher except for the use of brief quotations in a book review or scholarly journal.

rloweryhawk@gmail.com

Ordering information:

Special discounts are available on quantity purchases by corporations, associations, educators, and others. For details contact the publisher at the above address.

*Can also order single books from Author or Createspace.com

﹈ALSO BY R. LOWERY-HAWK﹈

- SPIRITUAL-PONDERING-ENLIGHTENING BOOKS: HELP BOOKS, NOVELS, POETRY, AND TEACHINGS

THE BOOKS OF "IS"
(BOOK ONE AND TWO)
---BOOK ONE: *The Dance of Becoming*
---BOOK TWO: *The Song of Sia, (in Progress)*

- *SCI-FI/FANTASY BOOKS: PONDER-ENLIGHTENING*

---NOVEL: *The Space Between the Worlds, VOLUME ONE: Zae-Bora-Zae-Boor,*
Earth's Sixteenth Dimension: *THE SHIFT*
(a work in progress)

UPCOMING:

- *SCI-FI/FANTASY-PONDER-ENLIGHTENING* BOOKS VOLUMES 2 - 7 of:
The Phoenixes, Thunderbirds, and Dragons-Atlantis Series

---BOOK TWO: Phoenixes, Thunderbirds, And Dragons: ATLANTIS,
Birthed by Fire and Water: THUNDERBIRD: Her Story
---BOOK THREE: Phoenixes, Thunderbirds, And Dragons: ATLANTIS,
Birthed by Fire, Earth, and Air: DRAGONS: *Their Story*
---BOOK FOUR: *Phoenixes, Thunderbirds, And Dragons: ATLANTIS,
Birthed By Heaven:* COMING TOGETHER: *Their Mission*

☙

- *PHOENIXES, THUNDERBIRDS, AND DRAGONS:*
Man's Legends
--- BOOK FIVE: *Legends and Stories of: THE PHOENIX:*
(Mankind's Preconceptions and Stories)

---BOOK SIX: *Legends: and Stories of: THE THUNDERBIRD:*
(Mankind's Preconceptions and Stories)

---BOOK SEVEN: *Legends and Stories of: THE DRAGON*
(Mankind's Preconceptions and Stories)

- **HOW TO BOOKS**

DEDICATION

I dedicate this to all Earth's children...

THIS BOOK IS DEDICATED TO NOT ONLY MY BIOLOGICAL FAMILY, BUT TO ALL CHILDREN, OF ALL AGES, THROUGHOUT THE AGES; BIOLOGICAL AND SPIRIT RELATED, WHO HAD BEEN HERE ON EARTH, ARE NOW HERE, AND, WHO COME HEREAFTER....

MAY YOUR JOURNEY BE POWERFULLY ENLIGHTENING, MOVING YOU UPWARD TOWARDS THE UNVEILING AND THE RELEASING THAT WILL LEAD YOU TO YOUR FREEDOM FROM THE MANIPUTIVE HOLOGRAPHIC ILLUSSIONS YOU HAVE BEEN EXPERIENCING. THIS I WANT FOR YOU, AND FOR ALL LIFE, THROUGHOUT ALL TIMES, AND ALL WORLDS ...

MAY YOU ACCOMPLISH THIS AND YOUR PURPOSE; EXPERIENCING JOY; AIDING ALL LIFE; WHILE RESTORING THE AWAKENING TOWARDS AND FOR,

THE ONE

ALSO,
In loving memory of: Dartanyon….
AND
Petey, Princess, Ninjinkia, Shadow, Keshia, Mia-1, Togan (Toggie), Motley, Missy, Mia-2, and Blackie…
Including just as important, the many others whom I have loved, and have loved me…

❧ CONTENTS ❧

UPCOMING BOOKS BY AUTHOR..3

DEDICATION……………….……..……………..………....5

ACKNOWLEDGEMENT……..………….……….......…9

INTRODUCTION……………………..……..................…11

QUOTE BY HERMANN HESSE...27

PROLOGUE POEM…..29

QUOTE BY PLATO..31

PHOENIX, HER STORY..33

DRAWING OF RAINBOW PHOENIX...................................34

QUOTE BY HAZRAT INAYAT KHAN..............................169

QUOTE BY ROBERT JUNGK...171

QUOTE BY ARISTOTLE..173

QUOTE BY OLIVER WENDAL HOLMES.........................175

LISTING OF THE SERIES...176

ABOUT THE AUTHOR………..…............................……178

CREDITS..179

ACKNOWLEDGMENTS

I WANT TO THANK:

- Daniel B., for his info and help in sending my book and cover to the publisher, via PDF and the internet.

- Paulette Winland, the additional info she had recently read about the Annunaki.

- And, all those who have researched and written about creation, legends, space visitors, and ancient civilizations; along with the various Culture's and their religions, stories, and beliefs. The research, studies, investigations, cultural histories, and oral stories passed down through the ages, enabled me to develop a great interest in researching more on these subjects, thus, resulting in my using in this book, what I have researched and learned.

Thank you!

INTRODUCTION

This book is a work of the imagination and documented finds from researchers of many of the subjects in this book. Therefore, this book bridges upon reality, and science fiction, but also on spirituality, legends, fantasy, and truth. This book also contains a few "tidbits" I've heard and read about over the last thirty-three years, on a variety of different cultural beliefs. It is also based upon my imagination and intuition. I have used information from the findings of several researchers of ancient texts and belief systems, along with archaeologist finds. The writings in this book were also created by my allowing me to flow with history, and myths, while attuning and connecting with my instinctive-natural-side of knowing; therefore, much of the story came from my visions, and "gut" feelings. Many then would say this is a book of fiction. Therefore read, enjoy, and ponder upon what you read, and then, *you* decide…

Yes, the stories within these books, written down by me, most likely will be thought, and consider, by many, to be friction…

FOR NOW…

*But*let*us*think*for*a*few*moments*

There have existed in the pass, many strange creatures, and many are still living among us *today*. There are Giraffes, Elephants, Hippopotamuses, and Ostriches; Platypuses, Manatees, Narwhals, and Flower Hat Jelly Fishes. There are also Tasmanian Devils, Thylacinus, Kiwi Birds, Rhinoceroses, Wombats, and Dinosaurs. And then there is the supposedly extinct, yet not, pangolin dragon! There are even more unusually strange and unbelievable creatures sharing the planet with us at this time besides these few I have mentioned. All real, and now known by mankind; living and thriving among us!

When we first discovered these unusual creatures, we most probably thought, when told of them, they were fiction and more like something more of a fantasy or out of a Sci-Fi novel rather than real. Yet, we accept them today as not only *really* existing, but as being perfectly normal in our world! Is it then too un-conceivable and unbelievable for us to except that Phoenixes, Thunderbirds, and Dragons might have existed among us…and perhaps *still* do? Myths and legends are stories, usually intertwined with truth and lessons woven through them, seeming too fanciful and too far out there to make sense; too confusing and beyond reality, as most of us understand reality to be, for us to believe the telling. Most myths and legends contain symbolic and metaphoric wordings, almost poetic in their relating, so to draw us in. Myths and legends are means of opening up the imaginative mind while also gently opening the intellectual mind to truths that are hidden from those they are meant to be hidden from, while they emerge into one's awareness, revealing themselves to those who recognize the "precious gems" that are lying within the supposedly mere "rocks" they seem deeply embedded in… thus, an example of a metaphor: comparing similar descriptions or definitions to help one to relate them to a deeper symbolic meaning, so to help one better understand, relate, and identify with what is being said. Myths, legends, and stories are entertaining, while they also take you on a journey outside the mundane world one lives in; depositing knowledge, wisdom, and lessons to the listener/reader, like seeds, awaiting their time to sprout and thrive; giving of themselves something important to others; (another example of a metaphor).

In writing this book I took in consideration, the legends, myths, Holy writings, beliefs and stories of the various cultures all over the world; plus discoveries, and speculations of many writers, researchers, and explorers from thousands of years back to present day. Some of these included were, the Native American's oral stories; Biblical text; the writings of the Sumerian; Mesopotamian; Egyptian; and Greek cultures; legends of mythical and mythical creatures from various parts of the world; plus various stories: children and adult alike, repeated down through the ages, all around the world for thousands of years! Were they just a mass imagination and fanciful mutual attraction? Or was there something these different cultures seen and experienced that lead them to tell these stories of strange magical-like creatures such as: the Phoenixes, Thunderbirds, and Dragons? And why do we find these creatures so fascinating? All over the world different cultures have passed down, for thousands of years, very similar stories about human-like reptilian people who created them and other species. But was the reptilian race actually reptile in appearance, or symbolic? Among these stories there are those about Phoenixes, Thunderbirds, and Dragons. When these stories from around the world are compared, they are all very similar, and, they all claim their stories are true! For example, their descriptions of "the thing" or "creature that came from the sky", varied from culture to culture, and personal sighting. The thing that came from the sky has been interpreted today as a meteor or comet. Their personal and limited sightings at that time, due to the relating of it to what they subjectively perceived, and felt it resembled, was usually from a familiar and known creature or object on Earth or from a created myth. The many religions all speak of a deluge: flood; and something fiery coming from the sky; describing it as a Serpent, Dragon, Meteor, or Comet; or, even the Devil…but could it have been a nuclear bomb? These cultures also speak of a drift and a time of darkness; living in caves; and coming forth from the Earth. Archaeologists and other researchers have found evidence of the Earth having a great change, a catastrophe, which caused a great loss of animal and plant life, along with a fire and great blast, ending the dinosaurs. Further research showed there was found signs of a great deluge; a drift of gravel, mud, fire, and ashes, which went on for hundreds of miles! A large boat, animal and human remains, the bones of fish, and bird; along with shells, pottery, woven mats and baskets, were found buried thirty and forty feet deep under gravel, rocks, stones, mud, and debris, and on land, near and far from the sea. Some of the skulls found were the skulls of giants! Some of those skulls were as tall as a man!

Cultures all over the planet held onto inter truths; protected, and kept from the masses. This was on purpose due to wanting to control and have power over the populace. We today, now have ancient writings, texts, and records from different ancient civilizations that speak of beings coming from the sky. Some of these beings were referred to as the Nephilim; the Giants; the Watchers; Fallen Angels; or the Annunaki; by the people of Mesopotamia and Sumeria: the 'gods' who came from the sky, around 450,000 years ago! Throughout the Christian bible, the term sons of God, was used to refer to celestial beings, referred to as Angels (messengers), or certain Giants. They also used the term Nephilim, a Hebrew word for giants, and literally meant the "fallen-down ones", (those who fell from the sky). (It has been said that the Annunaki were the off-springs of the Nephilim.) In the Old Testament they were known as: Rephaim, Anakim, Emim, Avim, Horim, and Zamzummim. Some scholars imagine that the tradition of mighty powerful demi-gods born from the union of gods and men is what formed the basics of the gods and demi-gods of Greek mythology. The Christian bible describes many of these tall hybrids as mighty men or heroes. The Sumerian culture is considered by most experts to be the cradle of civilization. It was thriving in an area called Mesopotamia, and flourished approximately 6,000 years ago! It was located in modern day Iraq and Kuwait, between two ancient waters of the Tigris and Euphrates rivers. The Sumerian ancient records maintain that for eons a cast of celestial beings, with multiple agenda, were here on Earth hundreds of thousands of years ago. They speak of two ruling brothers: Enki and Enlil, sons of the Lord/god Anu, who were in charge of a project. That project was: Earth! These Nephilim, and Annunaki, were master Geneticists, highly skilled in genetic organization and manipulation. They organized the genetic structures of life. Earth was like a laboratory for them to create new life forms and experiment on the life already here. The Annunaki were considered by some experts to be related to a reptilian (Serpent) race; plus, all over the planet people embrace the idea of Dragons or Serpents as the creators of life. Today our Scientists, and other great minds, have discovered that humans and reptiles have a common ancestor that dates back three hundred and twenty million years ago, referred to as the Amniocenteses. In the land known as Nag Hermedi, there was found, buried in clay vases, thirteen leather-bound papyrus books. Today these books are called the Nakamakodacees by a Christian group known as the Gnostics. These books were written in first century A.D. The texts in the books were written by Thomas, Phillip, and other biblical disciples. In these texts they speak of creatures called Arkons: human like reptilians.

It is said that the Nephilim knew the properties of gold and its frequencies, which came from a substance gold carries that is capable of opening portals/doorways to other dimensions! It is recorded that they, and their world's atmosphere, were in a great need for it, so they were also mining it for that purpose. The Sumerian and Egyptian writings say the way the Nephilim and Annunaki altered the DNA of our forefathers, the hairy indigenous human and ape like Hominids, who were living here at that time, was to take one of the four DNA codes from the Hominids, and change the base of that one cell's code; then they placed it in a female of the same species. But because the results of that created various deformities, they decided to try placing the single cell inside one of their own female gods instead. This change produced hybrids with no deformities. The perfected hybrids then were the result of being carried within a female 'god' as the mother, rather than a Homo-erectus or Hominid, and was said to have resulted in what we are today! The Sumerians say they called them/us: Adaptas! But, they created us not to be their children, but to use us for their slaves to work for them, especially to mine the gold! Some of the ancient writings found about the Nephilim, said they had an etheric body; and because Earth was not solid at that time, but was a planet of sound and water, which was solidifying into mass, they would no longer be able to mine the gold themselves, or they would be locked into a solid body form on Earth. They had first asked permission from the Atlantians to dig for the gold. The Atlantians were ethereal beings on Earth at that time. They were given permission. But when things began to solidify, the Nephilim decided to begin altering the indigenous hairy hominids. With the Atlantian's permission, they used the Atlantian's ethereal life force/selves, transferring them: the Atlantians, into the Hominid's bodies so they could use the solid bodies of the Hominids to do the physical mining for them, and the mental intelligence of the Atlantians to control the Hominids and communicate with them. All this may sound too fanciful and imaginative to believe...yet unusual things have happened before, over the thousands of years of mankind's existence, and found to be true! Could these strange reports and writings be true also?

All over the world various cultures speak of similar creation stories. The Greek have their stories of Greek gods who came from the sky. Their stories say these immortal gods divided the world among them. The continent of Atlantis was Poseidon's. Poseidon was said to have come from the sky and fallen into the sea, soon mating with a mortal Earth woman name Cleito. Some myths say he eventually turned into a half fish and half man. Poseidon and Cleito had five sets of twins, all male. Was this genetic engineering? Some think so! According to Plato's famous writings on Atlantis, Poseidon and Cleito's home was on a hill at the center of an Island, referred to as Atlantis. All ten of their adult sons were given a kingdom of their own to rule. Their first born was called Atlas. He was given the central temple on the highest point of the city. This temple was built around a mountain. There were five concentric rings, or motes of water; and land was dug, circling around the city. Two were land, and three were sea water. It is said warm and cold springs bubbled up from the Earth and they had them pumped into their homes. Channels were cut through the circles leading to the center core. Each one had land around it with forest. There was a stone wall protecting the central Island, it had a veneer of Orichalcum known as "Mountain Bronze", and gave off a soft glow like firelight when the sun shone on it! The temple had many golden statues. The largest was a god standing in a chariot driving six winged horses; around it were one hundred statues of sea nymphs riding on dolphins. The temple had pinnacles of gold and walls of silver. Outside the temple were gold statues of the king, his wife, their ten sons and their wives. The governing of the empire was in the hands of ten men. It is written that the Atlantians dealt fairly with others and lived in peace, but that the Divine within them began to grow dim because of their marriages with mortals. It then eventually died out. Their pride had grown, and they forgot their pledges! Ambition then overcame them, and they then reached for greater power! Atlantis was believed to be located in the region of the Americas, now covered by Peru and Mexico. The Mayans then, may be the decedents of Atlantis! Plato, a Greek Philosopher and poet, who lived three thousand years before Christ, said in his famous writings on Atlantis, that the continent of Atlantis was located pass the Pillars of Hercules, (the Strait of Gibraltar), which is the large land masses on each side of the gateway to the Atlantic Ocean and beyond. Peter Daughtrey, British Author of the book, Atlantis and the Silver City, and investigator of Plato's Atlantis writings, for over twenty years, believes Atlantis was located where Silves, of the

Southern Portugal area, is today. There are other Atlantis investigators who think Atlantis was located at Santorini, a neighbor of Akronn. Both places had been destroyed thousands of years ago by volcanoes, earth quakes, and flood, now rebuilt as Silves and Santorini. Some of these cities by the sea, have the same red white and black stones the Atlantians loved and built their walkways, statues, buildings, and many other things from. It is also said that Athen fought against Atlantis nine thousand years ago. Zecharia Sitchin, Writer; Alien and Ancient Astronaut Theorist; and Author of the book, "The 12th Planet", studied and researched the Sumerian language and their pictorial writings, then wrote of them in his book. The Sumerians talked of the gods, the Nephilim/Giants that came from the sky and altered the ape-man like creatures that lived here; creating the humans we are today! The Sumerians spoke of a catastrophe that destroyed all but a few of the new race called humans; humans who were told by Enki, and some say it was Marduk, to build a huge ship, so to save them and some of the other earth species, and some of the hybrid half-god children, plus the god's mortal wives, husbands, and the off-springs from their union. Save them from the flooding that was about to occur! Authors such as Immanuel Velikovsky, an investigator; and Eric Von Daniken, an investigator of Atlantis and Author of the book, "Chariots of the Gods", also writes of celestial astronauts, visitors from another world, who they think played a role in human history. Could the Atlantians have been some of the other worldly visitors who came and stayed? All of Mr. Daniken's and the other's findings, during their much researching and investigating, leaves one to believe in the real possibility that the ancient writings are true and not just made up stories for entertainment.

Join me now in the stories of a possible Atlantis, the visitors "from the sky", and three mystical creatures! Read *these mythical and legendary creatures'* stories...stories that tell the creature's side of the events in their lifetimes, and those of the Atlantians, its people, and those who came from another world! Stories that could be friction, or could *most probably* be true! Who knows what lies yet undiscovered, or what was, so many years ago, **before** man was created and then arrived to where he is today? Who knows of the events and creations, like stories, that happened and grew, over tens of thousands of years of time, when man had advanced in technology, then slid back to a more primitive state; there to begin, again: to perfect through changes brought on from selective breeding and earned experiences; and hopefully, this time, become both intellectually and spiritually more aware and caring of the delicate balance of life, succeeding at last, in breaking forth through the veil of illusions we all share? Being given another chance, would mankind slip back again or use his knowledge to better his self, the world, and all in it? Who knows for sure how the choices others made thousands of years ago, and even today, to one's self and to others, affected things and people then, and has affected creation today, and tomorrow; nor what higher life forms and creative life force/source, (what we might call God) may have intervened and done, or allowed, for a good reason, to be done! Perhaps all we can do *is* imagine! The imagination, the will, and the mind-full determination, are what create our achievements and helpful inventions. Imagination gives us much; included is hope, joy, and purpose. It motivates us to keep being a species, and to continue creating towards perfection; perfection that works for the betterment and **better** *of us* **all.** Through creating we climb that spiraling "ladder" of ascension to a higher knowledge, awareness, potential, and freedom; which are to lead us to the wisdom to assist others in their plight and struggle to climb it as well. The imagination links people together, making a stronger link of possibilities and achievements! There is much we have come to know, but there are even more we are yet to discover and learn. Perhaps *anything* **is** possible! And perhaps all we have to do is dream and imagine good and beauty, giving it life, and a chance to be! Imagination is one of our greatest gifts, so let us imagine for a moment: What *if* Atlantis and all these discoveries and reports are real? And what if Phoenixes,

Thunderbirds, and Dragons are real as well? If they could speak to us, would they share their adventures with us, taking us through time and history, seeing life through their eyes? It would be like we were time traveling on the wings of magical-like creatures; experiencing their powers, their life, their emotions, and their learned wisdom and enlightenment; and/or their darkness of hatred and loss of Soul. Yes, there would probably be some Phoenixes, Thunderbirds, and Dragons who had consumed themselves in darkness, filled with anger and hatred. Imagine how both of these types of creatures, "birthed by fire", might describe their own creation, their world, their feelings, thoughts, and their experiences, as they lived them. Wouldn't it be interesting to "hear" and see their side of the story, and not just the legends and myths created and told by the humans, according to *the human's* perceptions of what happened? Perhaps if you would allow your mind to go deeper into your imagination and join there with the metaphoric, spiritual, and the intellectual versions of the stories, you could perhaps travel through your psyche and discover great wisdom there that could heal the emotions and spiritual wounds you and the planet might have held buried from the pass, within you. Our mind, Spirit, and Soul loves the freedom of traveling to **beyond** the mundane present. Imagining can be a teacher, healer, and fun, as well as creative and resourceful! The Phoenix, Thunderbird, and Dragon, have lived on in many oral storytelling, books, and movies, as well as in our minds and our hearts. They shall now, in these four series of books, each tell their side of the story of *them;* taking you beyond the mundane of ordinary; allowing you to "fly" high with them on their personal journey "wings"; "seeing" through "their eyes"; "upon their wings"; and "through their mind", the world of them, and, of the long ago… In these stories you will learn not only their personal side of what has been told about them, but you'll also learn about personal individual perceptions, judged upon their limitations; about the Earth, the visitors from the sky, and the human race at that time. You will also learn of the ancient cultural creation stories, and catastrophically events, as well as the similarities these three legendary creatures share. You might gain wisdom; knowledge; and enlightenment; along with spiritual teachings,; plus, an important message these three creatures bring especially for you, and all that lives on this beautiful planet, Earth. Whether Phoenixes, Thunderbirds, and Dragons, among other "story-book", legends and mythical creatures, are simply symbolic and metaphoric tales of fiction, or are real, we can still learn from them by pondering upon what is written in this book and the future books under the same title; making these creatures a **possible good thing,** a good creation, rather than something to only fear or brush off and ignore! The Phoenixes, Thunderbirds, and Dragons in these four books, "tell their own story" to humankind…**to YOU**! They tell their thoughts, their emotions, their intentions, their experiences, and the reasons *why* and how they are, and *why* they did the things they did. They tell it to **you,** so you might **really** know them, and yourself; plus know the healing messages that they were told, by the higher power that sent them, and which the races of people on Earth need to know at this time in history. This higher power, of first cause of good and all creation, has directed them to tell human kind certain things which are necessary for their continuous existence. These three legendary creatures have woven their important massage/s and teachings into their stories, forming seed-codes for your gentle awakening. They know all this is important, and part of their mission, intended and designed from the Supreme Creator of all that is, that they share their story and its wisdom with you at this important time on Earth, so you can benefit from it in the way it embraces you, and you embrace it; then you are to share it with those you are called to share it with. These four special beings will, *together,* in the fourth book of this series, tell you why their stories are important, and why this is an important time on Planet Earth. They will then later come together to deliver to you the bigger part of their individual messages. But for now, perhaps all we can do is simply relax as you read their stories, and imagine what took place those hundreds of thousands of years ago; also give some thought about all the seemingly science fiction-like accomplishments and inventions man has made over the hundreds of years, and therefore, keep an open mind to the possibility of: celestial visitors, and the possible history of pass mysteries and creatures. Do we believe the discoveries and visual evidence we see, along with the recordings, testing, and various findings that have been discovered by the various Researchers, Investigators, Anthropologists, Archaeologists, plus, Historians, and many others? They and many others have done many years of research on these mysteries, recovering qualified evidence that these ancient tales may carry truths. Do we ignore all this and brush it off as fiction, along with the writings left behind from those who lived on Earth thousands of years ago, claiming truth? And do we say, "We have not experienced it, nor do we see such things in this day and age of any such creatures and happenings, therefore, they could not have, nor do they, exist?" It is for each of us to consider, and then decide for ourselves, if these things are true, and if things beyond modern day science, and our own experiences today, that seem like science fiction or fairy tales, could really have existed in a time other than now. There are many mysteries on the planet: the pyramids, crop circles, stone-hedge, and the giant standing stones found in Ireland, Britain and other parts of the world! These are only a small number of mysteries! Where did they come from? How were such large heavy stones lifted and placed in formations? And how were the crop circles and huge pyramids made? Who placed these huge wonders where they are, and how, and why? Even if you remain a skeptic...still it is a fascinating subject to imagine and consider. In this first volume, and its companion volumes, are stories using information from ancient writings, ancient cultural belief systems, ancient known spiritual truths, but also from my imagination and intuition. The writings also present deeper spiritual and ancient wisdom and knowledge. These volumes I have written are listed as science fiction-fantasy, but could things in these books be most probable, fringing on possibilities, containing many facts of truth? Or are the entire stories merely fiction and imagination? I leave it to you to decide what is fiction or truth. **You** be the judge…your Divine Spirit, along with your Soul, and your inner knowing, will be your guide… Read this series as a curiosity and enjoyment, with things to ponder upon; for these stories are written for your enjoyment, but also for your consideration; relating; education; enlightenment; and assistance toward freedom from the holographic illusion… They are also for your DNA de-coding, for the awakening of your conscious awareness, to free you up to accomplish all that…thus, maybe then, even an elixir of light for your stored memories…

I hope you enjoy The Rainbow Phoenix's storytelling. It is **her** gift to all life. Sharing it, is **my** gift to you…I hope you will embrace, in a good way, the stories these ancient legendary creatures are sharing with you; always keeping your heart, mind, Spirit, and imagination open; focusing on the truth and the good of, and for: creation. For then ***anything is*** possible! And with love, patience, hope, empathy, imagination, faith, forgiveness, and compassion, for life, self, others, everyone, and everything, along with its benefits, you will then "grow wings"; be "fired" up; "break free"; and "fly"! …Spreading your wings, like, the fiery,

Phoenixes, Thunderbirds, and Dragons!

Enjoy!

--- DR. R. Lowery-Hawk ---

*Many believe the Phoenix and the Thunderbird are related to the Hawk…

This book and its companion books are listed under Sci-Fi-Fantasy. But could things in these books be most probable, containing many facts of truth? Or is it merely fiction and imagination? You be the judge. Read and ponder...the pondering may give you the answers...

Books are only a value when they lead us towards life
and serve and benefit the living. Every hour spent
reading is wasted if the reader does not experience a
spark of energy, a presentiment of rejuvenation,
an idea of new life.

---Herman Hesse---

"I hope this book does that for you..."

---R. Lowery-Hawk---

PROLOGUE POEM
"PHOENIXES, THUNDERBIRDS, AND DRAGONS"

THEY SHALL TELL YOU A STORY,
OF A TIME BEYOND THE SEA;
OF THINGS THAT CANNOT EXIST,
YET COULD ALSO POSSIBLY BE---

Open your Spirit, open your mind as well;
Let your imagination soar,
As you travel these magical tales ---
They're wrapped in light, seemingly like impossibilities;
Judge for yourself, but imagine and think;
Get the full feel of these ---
For each of us have our experiences, their truths we define;
Each moving, there living,
Wrapped up in our own mind ---
Many story worlds are created;
Their readers they do find;
For the stories are Soul related,
Drawing the intended, at the right time---
And so then it is, each of us must decide,
The world we'd like to visit;
The someplace else, we'd like to *sometimes* reside ---
These are such adventures, Castled forth to take you there;
To the land of "not's and maybe's", while you imagine,..
And your wishes grant you fair---

SO ENJOY AND DREAM,
LET YOUR IMAGINATION GROW 'WINGS",
SOAR UPWARDS IN YOUR MIND,
AND SHARE THE GOOD THEREIN YOU FIND ----

SOMEONE WHO ISN'T CONVINCED
OF SOMETHING HIMSELF
WOULDN'T BE CONVINCED ABOUT IT
BY YOU EITHER.

---PLATO-

VOLUME ONE

"BIRTHED BY FIRE"

THE PHOENIX...

Her story…

your beginning?

THESE SERIES ARE BOOKS OF CODES FOR THE ACTIVATION OF YOUR ENCODED TRUTHS---

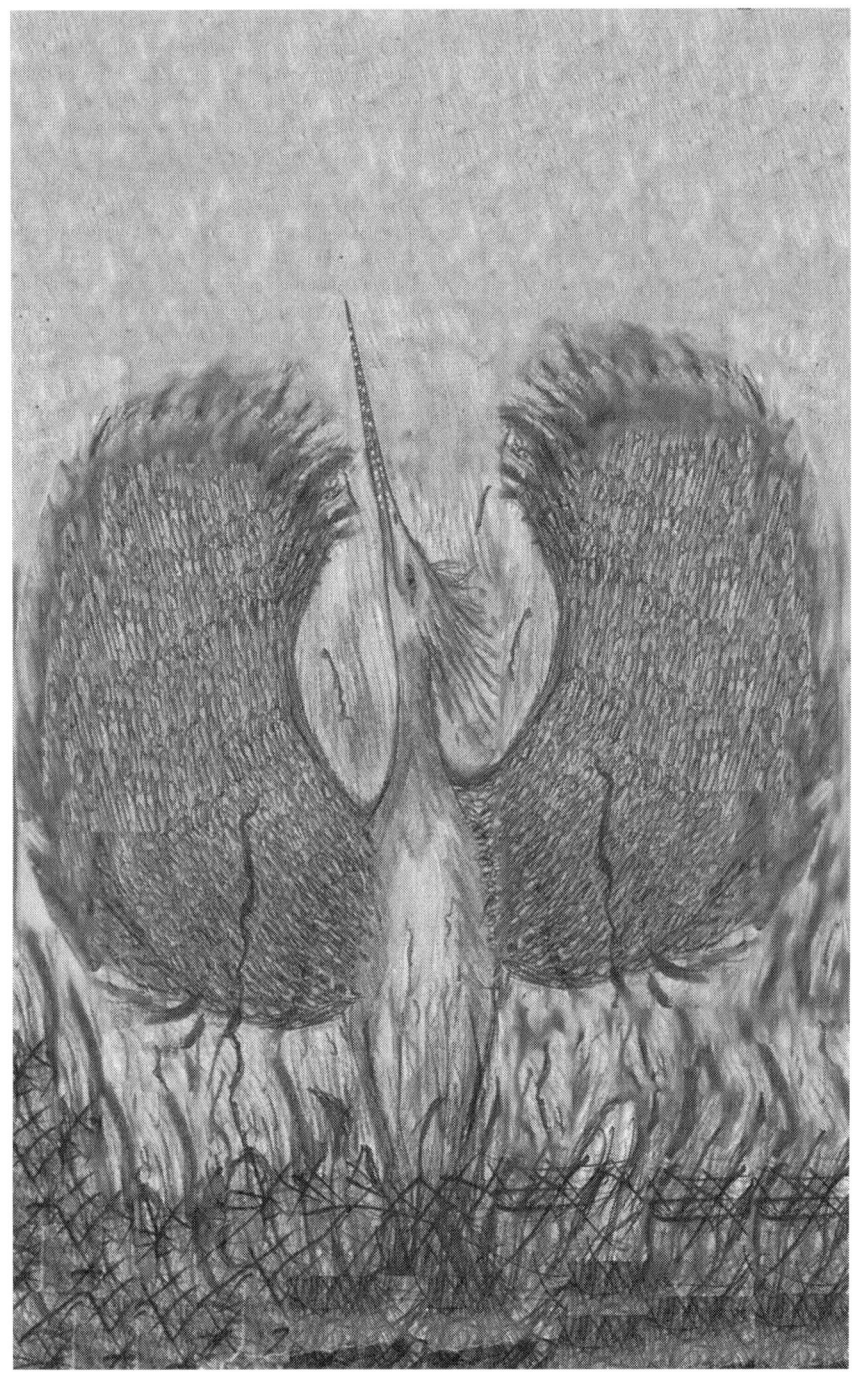

PHOENIX, RISING OVER ATLANTIS...

"I am Tii-Us, the She-Phoenix of Atlantis.

"THE FIRST"...

There have been many stories told of my kind; told and retold over countless years. Some carry much truth, while others are only told from another's perspective and conception.

I HAVE MY STORY TO TELL...
A story about me, and my truths of all that involved me; a story of my actions and others; and how they affected me, you and other life;
This story is a story of how I became known as,

THE SHE-PHOENIX THAT ROSE OVER ATLANTIS...

And, it is the story of **you**...

My story I have carried within me for times lost and times found; times un-measurable by your human capabilities. But once, during my time of long ago, the Earth's alien non-humans and half human off-springs, not only measured time, but were learning how to controlled it! But I am getting ahead of myself. Let it be known that my story has pained me for what seemes like more than eons of time...and yet, I also smile at times, when I think upon that continent known as Atlantis... I smile because though it was the cause of my sadness it was also the cause of my, at last, happiness... I shall now begin un-spinning the tale that I've carried and wrapped around me for so long...

There are many stories living on within us; life's stories, living on in the fruit of the tree of life, within the spiraling double-ladder of the DNA. Some stories have special meaning, but mostly only personal, only useful, so many think, only to those who came up with them, and not to anyone else. Although, in truth, *everyone's* stories of their personal experiences with life have *great* meaning to *everyone and everything!* They are more important than most realize. Then…there are stories of a grander and nobler cause; and of a more important and universal purpose and meaning to *everyone and everything! I* have such a story to tell…

Sat or lie comfortably now. Relax as I unwind my story's message of truth and wisdom of a great importance to *you*. My story comes from the very depth of my being, in the 'hall' of life's records, stored within me, within the Earth, and within the Heavens; stored there since the beginning of time, *before* mankind existed. They were put there by the Eternal One/s: the Eternal Mother/Father who shines for, and in, **all things**, **creating *all* things**. They are stored within the Earth and in *you* as well. You but have to *earn* the right, by your experiences, will, and desire; and learn the correct way to access them.

These histories of life and creation I have, I can, and **am**, *permitted* to tell, for I am Tii-Us, the ancient one; the flaming *first* Phoenix who has mastered, and *is of* the multiple color spectrum of this world! I am therefore the Rainbow Phoenix, conceived by the fire, and re-birthed by the light. Mutated flier was I; man and god created; flaming and fire risen: Phoenix re-created by the Supreme Eternal One/s: God of all Gods! I was re-born out of fire and ashes; from pain and pleasure… and the old ones refer to me as:

The Rainbow Phoenix who rose over Atlantis…

"I begin my story with the events and the sights of that majestic great city Atlantis, along with her people who lived there. I begin this telling in the age before the Thunderbird

and the Dragon of Earth existed; before man existed; because I am the first! My story begins even before me and my legend began. The story I am about to tell you, therefore, begins before the people began weaving their stories, legends, and myths about me, my-kind, and the Thunderbird and Dragon!"

The Great She-Phoenix paused a few moments in a place of stillness as if remembering and reminiscing once more; experiencing her life there in the ancient age of Atlantis. A smile began slowly forming at the mouth of her large pointy beak. Her smile revealed two rows of very sharp tiny teeth, making her appear more fierce and dangerous, like the Pterodactyl, the flying bird-like dinosaur, rather than peaceful and joyful as she really felt at this moment. Thinking upon the good in her pass, was what made her smile. Her two large hearts beat calmly, yet powerfully strong in her multicolored scaled and feathered chest. Her chest rose and fell as great gust of air was pulled into and out of her lungs, sounding with a melody... a song, moving through her large nostrils. She now begins again sending her story-thoughts outward to the human race. These thoughts are the story she is sharing with us. This telepathic way of telling her story also ensures that her story reaches only the *human* race, for there are many other races of beings abound, and not all good. She especially wants to reach those humans who need extra help in reaching their human potential. Some of the human race has reverted back in their evolution, which is set forth by, and through, the Eternal Shinning One/s of all things. Those spiritually lost humans have become beings of much mindless chatter and drifting lost ways of existing. It is these she especially wants to help awaken. The thought particles she sends are too tiny, and their frequencies are too high, to be seen or heard by the human eyes and ears of today. But the human mind of today is still capable of receiving words and pictures telepathically. Symbols, recorded deep within creation's "tree of life" could reach them, and so were also being used.

The Phoenix's story-thoughts of her knowledge and experiences of the ancient city of Atlantis, and of her part in it, first began thousands of years ago while the human race had slept. This was the first step in getting her story to us and releasing the embedded light codes within us. Telepathic thought-particles were used while we slept because thought-particles are easier to be received by us, and drawn to us, while we sleep. Particles are drawn like a magnet to the deep electrical calmness that only sleep can provide, while the Soul travels. The Soul would then meet with the Fire-Bird: the Phoenix, while the thought light particles penetrated the memory cells, ensuring that humans received her story on **all** levels. She says she has been sending the human race her story for a very long time, while we slept; and now the next level to reach us is through the reading of it. These different levels are required to embed the information into the receiver: us, to aid in the awakening of the God-DNA. This DNA is encoded as a blue print within the Human race by the one and true God of **all** creation. This story the Phoenix is to share with us also lives on in the particles stored within us. Her story living within us is awaiting to begin again, just as the Fire-Bird, many times called: the Phoenix, had rose upwards to new heights and awareness, and into re-birth; into renewal of the mind, Spirit and Soul so to assist humankind into reaching their full potential in a correct and harmless way. She asked permission, from the great Eternal One/s, to be allowed to assist in mankind's renewal, the re-birth of the super human: the children of the mighty Eternal Shinning One/s! The She-Phoenix and the Eternal One/s want us to have this other chance; allowing us another attempt at perfecting ourselves and the entire human race, with compassion, but also including perfecting the human Soul, while disciplining the human nature.

The Rainbow Phoenix blinks her huge, slanted eyes that shine iridescent with reddish-gold. Traveling backwards in her mind to the long ago time of Atlantis, she begins again to share with

you her story as *she lived and* remembers it...

"The city of Atlantis was grand, and what you of today might refer to as, magical! Magical because the city and its structures were not only tall, but scientifically created and constructed to be able to not only house the Atlantians comfortably and well protected from the elements, any intended harm, and any invasion from the ground, sea and air, but also for its beauty to the eyes. Their city magically sparkled with color and could be viewed by them at all times, whereas it could be also dimmed in beauty when needed to provide concealment from others. The city, at times itself seemed alive, shimmering, and pulsating pale, iridescent blue, and violet in the light of day, like a beating heart with its colors moving with it in a slow rhythmic dance! At night this marvelous and strange city seemed to blend into the darkness, and disappear to all those who might chance upon her island. But, inside, the lights lived!

The Atlantians powered many machinery and instruments with fire-quartz crystals. They also had the knowledge of atomic power and anti-matter, among much other scientific advancement. They knew how to split the atom, and how to set protons to moving to create worm holes and anti-matter! And, with the anti-matter, they lit their entire city!

There were large white stone buildings, but most of their buildings were made from the blue, red, black, and white rocks they found, and were attracted to, on the islands. Many of the columns of their buildings were inlaid over with gold, and a special copper-gold they had mined from the mountains. Some of these columns were inscripted, much like the tablets they had mounted on their walls. These tall columns stood in front of the palaces that housed the ten ruling Pharaohs/Kings, and their Queens. The ten sons of the elder, first King, when adults, had each been given the position of a King with his own kingdom to rule with his wife and descendants. This first original King was said to have come from the sky then entered the sea (from the planet Sirius?), and was half man and half fish. He is said to have had five sets of male twins; and so there were ten ruling Kings in Atlantis at this time. And that was the way Atlantis ruled ever after that: Ten Kings and ten kingdoms, with ten governors.

The desire for columns and other architectural designs for their buildings and cities, were created not only from the memories the king and the others from the other world had of the buildings from their home planet, but the desires also came forth from their encoded ancestor's memories that were stored in their cells and DNA/chromosomes. Their chromosomes, and every cell of their body, contained the storage of their ancestor's memories and their love for this form of architecture. In their architect they had embedded precious and semi-precious gems which they brought from their home world, but also those they found in the Earth, her caves, and even the sea. They embedded these gems into the pillars that were also inside the buildings. There were especially inlaid in these pillars, stones and metals of Lapis Lazuli, carnelian, amethyst, ivory, gold, silver, brass and copper, to name a few. Their doors were double doors, inlaid with silver, copper and gold. Their High Priests and Priestesses wore blue robes and beautiful head dresses with smaller pieces of these same metals and gems; and among them were tiny geometric cut metals, polished so smooth that they were mirrors, re-flexing light and all that was around! Their robes and headdresses were also designed with feathers of various colors.

Some called this city the copper or brass city, while others referred to it as the city of gold and light, or the city of ivory. The Atlantian-Annunaki had built a great tall wall around the islands they had built their city upon. There were several other islands, in a large circle, surrounding the city. There were also three rolls of earth structures around the city for protection. In between them were canals. They could fish there, swim there, and store their canoes there. There were gates they could open to allow exit or entry to the canals, so their canoes could take their slaves or them to a neighboring island. There the slaves would go to the islands to grow and harvest food; chop and gather wood; dig for medicines and minerals; or slay an animal for its meat.

The city had massive library halls that rose upwards to sixty feet or more! These massive libraries contained some books made and bound like yours are today; but they also had scrolls hand written by scribes on special reef parchment! These were rolled up and stored in metal elongated cylinders to preserve them. Because they were a race of high technology, introduced by a more advance race that had come to the Earth from another world, and many still ruling and living there, they had the tools and the knowledge to provide things for themselves that you of today would think were magical, un-believable, and perhaps un-conceivable! Most the Atlantians were not only from that alien gene pool, but the Rulers, and those who governed the city, were from other worlds still living and controlling the city! The others were hybrids...off-springs, from the aliens! The Atlantians were beings of an etheric energy! But the indigenous hairy Hominids: ape-like humanoid, were of mass substance! The Aliens who visited the Earth thousands of years ago, were called the Nephilim and the Annunaki and were giants! They traded with, and eventually used and controlled the Atlantians. The Annunaki requested the Atlantians help them with the creating of workers to mine gold, by allowing their Atlantian's ethereal selves to inter the ape-like people. They wanted to help, so they agreed to this! In exchange, the Nephilim taught them many things about technology...but they also taught them some of their secrets on alteration of cells/chromosomes, and genes/DNA engineering. The Atlantians were then able to invent many marvelous things because of the advance technology they learned from the Nephilim, Annunaki, the Sirians, and the Reptilian people! Some of these inventions were used in the large libraries of Atlantis! What was mostly used and placed in their libraries were put on forth inch, round, or rectangle shaped microrecording disks that one could insert into either a wide clip that could be worn looped over the ear; if it was only audio. It could also be inserted, like the video recordings were, into a small four inch machine that could be set on a flat surface, a button pushed, and a hologram of words or/and images, moving or standing still; then would be projected, three dimensional, as if what stood before them were really there! They could push a top button to project the image straight up, as if the image was standing on top of the box, or push the side button to project the hologram outward and from the side, or in front of them! There could be sound, or not, accompanying these holograms. These holograms of people could voice what a book or scroll might only have words to read. These projections made what one viewed seem very real and life-like, so this method was usually preferred over reading from scrolls or books by most of the Atlantians. They also knew how to use quartz crystals to communicate and transport to the celestials.

Their huge city was also created to house them comfortably in *all ways* needed and desired; not just to survive, but to entertain and be entertained; but mostly to enjoy and make life easier to do so! Therefore, their buildings were built to provide splendid views of the city, the sea, and the sky and heavens! The city had a metal dome of thick and diamond hard metal that could close in the city if they were to be attacked by enemies; but also for protection if threatened by the sea or the elements. There was also created a smaller dome that was a building in its self. When the domed top was closed they could have the heavens enlarged by their magnifying equipment that re-produced the huge outside telescope's view of the heavens, and could then project it in the moment, onto the dome ceiling inside! When the dome was open, the heavens could be viewed from the sky as seen by the naked eye! The Atlantians had an extraordinary, and huge telescope that could pick up not only the sight of the further away star, planet, or constellation, but could also pick up the sound they made: each individual one! This then could be sent and projected to the indoor dome which held many comfortable reclining chairs for the people to rest in, so to view and hear the enlarged heavens! The images could be projected in larger or smaller sizes so those of the city and its scholars could study them, or simply be mesmerized by them, seeing the heavens as diamonds of light; and in hopes too, that they might see their star relations returning! These telescopically projections were live, seen in true time, projected every night, and viewed whenever anyone pushed a release button that was inside the dome, and, or, went to the telescope! This would then release whatever the huge outside telescope viewed to the overhead dome inside! This telescope constantly viewed the heavens in a slow sweep.

The city of Atlantis had Healers, and Plant Communicators, Gardeners, Herbalists, Mid-Wives, and Oracles, besides their Scholars, Scientists, Geneticists, Teachers, and other various experienced and knowledgeable teachers and workers. They all had different degrees of the knowledge and wisdom from their ancient ancestors, from the stars. This was all passed down through their DNA. Those first four mentioned were the ones who saw to it that the Atlantians were provided the most nutritional foods and water. The Herbalists were the ones who provided the healing plants, if the need arose, for they were trained not only in the healing abilities of the plants, but also the body's functions and needs! The Herbalists sometimes worked with the Pant Communicators and Garden-nesses before choosing the plant best required for pacific healings. There was seldom a need for them by Atlantian-Annunaki, but the need was often for their slaves! This was true because the Atlantians were the ancestors of the Nephilim people who came from the sky! Many still living in the city called Atlantis! The sky people were referred to as gods; and also they were called the Annunaki, Nephilim, the watchers, giants, or fallen Angels. They came to Earth from a planet called Nibiru, located beyond Neptune, but in the same solar system as Earth. Some even say they came from the Pleiades, Orion, and Sirius.

It took the Nephilim's elliptical planet, Nibiru, 36,000 years to reach

Earth's inter-solar system so they could be close enough to journey to Earth. This was the year many refer to as 2024 BC.

Atlantis city was a city build from thousands of years of knowledge, on all levels, from the combining of the Nephilim, and the already existing intelligent race of humans already living here on Earth at that time: the ethereal Atlantians! Since they were ethereal, they would appear invisible to those who were solid. Atlantis became a city of super human giants of mixed bloods and pure bloods of various heights! These beings were considered giants when compared to the size of Earth's humans today! Because of their knowledge of health and longevity, the giants not only lived for hundreds of years, but also rarely became unwell! The city depended a lot on the Holy Ones: the Priests, the Priestesses, Oracles, and the Healers; but they also depended upon the Herbalists; Plant Communicators; and Gardeners. The Scholars, Inventors, Geneticists, and Scientists were right up there with them in being deemed, not only of value, but also, the 'tap root', and the core of their culture and their magnificent city! The large city always had ten Rulers: Pharaohs/Kings and Queens. Each one had their own symbol and its symbolic way of ruling and engaging their own abilities. These abilities were gained from their personal experiences and choices, and what they learned and earned from them. They drew upon their symbol's power and the star they were born under and mastered. They also drew upon the plant, stone, and creature symbols that best suited them and their ruling! They had a principle law; an original, natural, and ancient law, that lived on within them and was genetically passed on to their descendants! This law stood for *who* they were, and *what* they were; and what they could be capable of. It was a law that was, to them, more of a *natural and sensible* way of living then it was an actual law. The law **was** them! This law therefore, *all* the rulers honored, believed in, and upheld! It was ingrained within them through their Star Relation's gene pool! For them **everything** had to have order and purpose; focused upon perfection; striving to be God-like in knowledge, potential, and power! This law was referred to as: The Law of Mastery and Perfection! This law stated that improvement was **always** possible, and entitled one, and demanded one to master **all** limitations and weaknesses! This law said: if one could prove he or she out-mastered the others in whatever they attempted to master, they could then come before the counsel as an important and respected elder, or even possibly join the counsel of those who governed the city, assisting in the city's ruling. It also stated that s/he who dreams a 'dream' of improvement should do all to create it and experience it, and, therefore, learn from it and master it! After doing so, that one is a true demi-god: the master and creator of his achievement/s even if it were but only an improvement on the self and no one else chose to learn from what he had accomplished! To not strive to this law is stagnation and decay; a disease that could infect their *entire* race, for all is transferred to future generations! Not following the law also meant, to them, a forgetting and disrespect of their ancestors, and it was then an insult, dishonoring the ancestors, and also **all** their descendants! If that were done, one is so polluted that he or she must be re-located to another more distant island to live out their years; for to stay meant a possible contamination of their gene pool by way of others following the same pattern; thus a toxin/disease passed on to future generations, setting them back thousands of years! The Atlantians, The Watchers, called: The Giants, or The Annunaki, by many of the islanders, had inherited the results of their alien ancestor's thousands of years of selective breeding; and it was therefore, **now their** responsibility to keep up the traditions and keep the gene pool pure in certain matters! *No matter what* may be, or appear to be, cruel in doing so! This that they had learned, earned, and accomplished, were gifts bestowed upon them by the high gods from their ancestors! Bestowed upon them *intentionally* so that their off-springs might reap an even grander life than they had lived! Because of this they became an advanced race, culture, and civilization; bringing forth this great city from what they had available on Earth, and what they had brought from their own world! They used what they had available and pulled on the gifts of their ancestor's knowledge embedded in their DNA, to survive and continue their ways and laws of existence here on Earth.

This city of Atlantis existed on a large island, surrounded by a circle of smaller islands. These islands were located in the Atlantic Ocean, the Green Sea, as many referred to it; pass the "Pillars of Hercules", (the straits of Gibraltar) and close to the Mediterranean. Atlantis lied approximately where the Antarctica is today and close to Japan; South Africa; Central America; and the Bermuda Islands.

When the Nephilim, Annanaki, along with the Atlantians, began to settle on their islands, there were Native tribes who already lived there. They were captured and turned into slaves to do the bidding of the Nephilim and Annanaki! They were also used to experiment on, al-tering their chromosomes and DNA! The Annunaki were giants! Some thirty plus feet tall; and through inter breeding and genetic engineering many of the Atlantians therefore became giants! They were then much stronger than the native islanders, and had high technology which the tribes did not! Therefore, the natives were easily and quickly conquered! The native slaves were divided up and given to the Rulers of each ruling sector of the large city. The Rulers there then divided the slaves up again and gave them to the At-lantians who assisted the city and its people the most, such as the Scientists, Geneticists, Gardeners, Healers, Midwives, 0racles, and those who cared for the children of the Rulers. It was the slaves that went to the islands every day to gather fresh spring water for the Atlantians and their pets to drink, bath in, and to water their gardens. The slaves also grew and harvested fruits; nuts; seeds; and vegetables, off the Islands. They also fished and slayed animals for the At-lantian's food; cut wood, and dug for the precious minerals and metals in the hills; caves; oceans; and the flat ground! The Atlantians had also grown smaller gardens of foods and flowers in, and around the court yards for the people to help themselves whenever they so desired. This too were weeded and cared for by slaves; but also by one sec of the Atlantian's Gardeners called: Garden-nesses. These were women who had great knowledge and intuition on how to produce the fruits and vegetables with the most nutritional and medicinal value. Also, the Herbalists; also women, had their own section of ground set aside for the growth of herbs, both culinary and medicinal, for *all* the people. These plants were grown around their homes, sealed off from the public due to the strong medicinal power that had to be guarded and given out carefully; but only when needed; unlike the fruits, nuts, and vegetables that could be freely, and often, eaten.

The city was divided into castes. The first and highest caste was, of course, the Rulers: the Pharaoh Kings, Queens, and their families. The next circle of importance consisted of the caste of those who worked with the Soul/Spirit, and those who worked with the mind. The Scientists, Geneticists, and Scholars were keepers and developers of the mind and body; whereas the Healers, Herbalists, Garden-nesses, Priests/Priestesses, and Oracles, were the guardians and keepers of the faith: Holy Ones, care-takers of the Spirit for the Soul, as well as for the body! And still yet, these Holy people, at first, accepted and saw nothing, or little, wrong with making slaves out of the indigenous people of the surrounding islands! They, and most of the Atlantians condoned even more contradiction things, as you will soon learn! But that was in the beginning...

Atlantis and its people were thriving and doing very well; but the majority of the city's Ruling Kings, Scientists, and Geneticists were strong in their desire to try *new* things. The Atlantians had been very peaceful and fair people. But after the Annunaki involvement things changed due to unexpected results of their agreement to allow some of their Atlantian people to merge into the ape-like Hominids: primitive indigenous people, bodies, who lived on Earth at that time. The people the Atlantians merged with, eventually took on the intelligence of the Atlantians; and they eventually evolved more like the Annunaki, due to the alterations of their chromosomes, and the DNA of the Annunaki. They also became curious of what they could do and create; for the knowledge from the Annunaki was great, and they were now capable of much! The Atlantian's own alien DNA was already very knowledgeable; and with the alien Annunaki influence, it compelled them with extreme confidence, and genetic ruling, to desire to perfect and master! Plus, they had begun to develop greed; wanting more and more of *all* they *could* imagine! Their ability to create high technology added to their ego, becoming one of selfishness, over confidence, along with their belief they had *earned the right* to perfect, master, and control *all* on Earth! Like the Annunaki, they began to believe the planet was theirs alone! That was what they had convinced themselves to believe, and how they justified themselves and whatever they did! The Annunaki later began using the Atlantians to help them create workers out of the ape-like people, and alter many of the life forms on Earth! So the Atlantians became altered as well, in thoughts and belief systems, and eventually begun believing they were also superior to *all* people and *all other life* on this planet! For those advanced alien off-springs who lived here at that time saw no other life forms that could compare to them in *any way*! And so, the next step, they felt, was to 'improve upon creation' like the Annunaki were doing; *and take* control of it! These ways were approved by the Rulers of the city because in the Kings and Queens way of thinking, it was allowing their Geneticists and Scientists a 'hobby', while also providing a study of perfection in their race's evolution of awareness on life. It was something they believed would greatly benefit them, their people, and their Geneticists and Scientists! It would be fun, interesting, and knowledgeable, they thought, for these specialists and for them as well to see what **could** be created! In the process it would eventually satisfy *all* their in-born curiosity! The Ruler's thinking was, that they, themselves, would also have some-thing to look forward to while they waited to see what the knowledge of their ancestors, stored within their gene-pool, by way of their Scientists and Geneticists, could create and master from the life forms they had available on this planet! So the Earth became a laboratory for improving on all life, in their way of thinking. Therefore, the Rulers **all agreed to allow** the alteration of the Earth's creatures, including the Earth's humans!

In their single minded greed and desire for the growth of their minds, and what they could think to create, they began to lose 'sight' of their Soul's Divinity! They forgot to remember the one-plus-one-rule of the planet Earth, this world. The one-plus-one-rule is what governs this planet, keeping it functioning for survival, and keeping it in the most pleasant way for all life here; keeping it balanced and continuing! One of the rules of Ones is the World of Nature…the World of Matter; things appearing tangible and real to other life here! The other One is the Spirit that lives within this world, and within *all the life here*, below, and above; all connecting with all worlds into all creation, and on to the source of its Spirit and its Soul: the Soul of the *One Soul of* **all creation: the All of ALL**! Because they concentrated more on things of the mind, and ignored more the things of the Divine; the mind, Spirit, and Soul were then divided, and therefore, not of a 'single eye' of the Eternal Light, referred to by many of you, as the first creating God of all that is! Rather than keeping their Spirit and Soul pure, while engaging in the mind, they ignored the Sacredness and the One-plus-One-rule this world, and most worlds, operates on! Because of this rule, this dimension is able to keep on existing! This rule they forgot, for they believed they could master even *that*! Master and control the planet's perfect balance and it's sharing with *all other things* that existed here; so drugged they became with themselves, their thoughts, and their desires of power! When the Holy Ones learned that the Scientists and Geneticists were going to experiment on the humans, using other life species to create stronger slaves, the Holy Ones tried reasoning with the Rulers and with the Scientists and Geneticists. They tried desperately to remind them all of the Sacredness and the back-slap that happens when the Sacredness of mind and emotions is not working with the Sacredness of the Spirit and Soul! They reminded them of what kinds of dangers can, and have, occurred because of imbalance and greed! They reminded them that destruction of everything on the planet Earth could possibly happen, spreading all across the land, creating even more disasters when the planet tries to desperately re-set the balance of her world! They reminded them that it would cause a ripple-effect that would extend to other worlds disrupting its frequencies, creating a rip in time! The fabric of the other worlds then would be ripped, resulting in disasters and the swallowing up of other worlds! But the Rulers and the Scientists and the Geneticists argued that it was the natural next step and would help them all, and everything would be okay. They said they had control over what they did, and so they would, and could, control whatever happens. They even quoted the law of mastery and perfection to those who advised them to stop and consult with their Spirit that lives in them, and connects them to their Soul and the Eternal One God/s, the true and original Creator! But they clung to the law of mastery and perfection; using it to justify all that they wanted to do! The Holy Ones were losing ground, for those that ruled the city sided with the Scientists and Geneticists! Those against it went to the Oracles, pleading their case to them, asking for their sight on what could come to be if the Scientists and the Geneticists continued with their plans. The Oracles began moving into their trance state to see the future and what it held. They soon began to glimpse images, but scattered and hazy, moving about quickly, like dark clouds and speeding lights; then darkness, heat, cold; things not clear enough, with evidence for them to go up against the Rulers! They were frightened of the Rulers, but also, they confided in confidence, they felt fear rising within them of a stronger force, for they sensed many changes were about to happen; things that moved the Cosmic Seas, giving them a sense of a great upcoming turbulence! These things brought about great fear and concern to the Oracles! They too felt the experimenting should be stopped until further consulting with the Unseen Ones, who work with the Eternal One/s, could be done! But still, they would not go before the Rulers…until it was too late...

Soon, animals of various kinds were captured and taken to the Scientist's labs! They had first chosen smaller animals for their experimentation, but ones who had abilities and traits they themselves found desirable to reproduce! They then began exchanging DNA from one to the other, choosing those characteristic traits which they felt would combine well together and produce the results they wanted! They came up with some very unusual species! There had not been, at that time, a lot of varieties of species on this home planet of yours, not until they began their experiments of re-creating the life forms they found here. Some experiments went badly, killing the specimens, many times in excruciating agony! Some of the more successful alterations produced creatures who were either insane with madness and violence, or were staggering idiots, not capable or not knowing, how to stand, eat, nor drink! These they destroyed and threw out to the sea to be devoured by the huge water creatures that lived there! It was a pitiful and sorrowful sight, for those of a more compassionate Spirits witnessing this! Yet, it is what first invoked the compassion in those who were now beginning to oppose these things. It even brought out compassion in some of the Geneticists and Scientists! The Healers and Holy ones sought council with the Rulers of their city to voice their concerns, but they were denied that opportunity! Those Scientists, and Geneticists, who had felt compassion for these poor creatures being altered, now voiced their concerns to their Kings, wanting to find another more compassionate means of perfecting! *For wasn't this the purpose?'* they asked the Rulers and fellow Scientists and Geneticists, *'to perfect, so the creation could have a better existence, aiding **all**?'* But they were overruled by the majority. The Scientists and Geneticists who wanted to continue with their experiments justified it, appeasing their conscience by telling them-selves, and those who were concerned, that what they do *is* for a greater good and cause; and that all they needed to ensure this would work was to mix a bit of *their* own DNA strain with the creatures they were re-creating! 'Hadn't their ancestors, the Nephilim,' they said, *succeeded in their creation of the improved humans they had experimented on when they had first came to this planet and had mixed some of their own DNA with the lesser evolved beings; including* *their other ancestors, the Atlantians?* The hairy humans then, at that time, stood on two legs, but were more like the other hairy animals that inhabited this planet. You refer to them today as Hominids. Those Hominids, at that time, ran with the gazelles and other wild four legged creatures! Only they mostly ran on two legs, and were more in use of their hands and minds in creating and making decisions. They would show compassion by releasing the traps the Nephilim would set, which were meant to capture animals alive to experiment on or to eat.

The Nephilim-Annunaki's experiments eventually were successful, resulting in producing the more aware and intelligent human of today. They then believed the missing link for their new creations were in their *own* DNA that now contained the DNA of the Nephilim and the Annunaki! After the Atlantians found success in experimenting on animals, birds and reptiles, they began again on the humans! They decided to create worker slaves of great strength, but loyal and obedient to the ones who created them! Ones who weren't too smart, but smart enough to follow commands, and do the tasks set before them; and, as equally in importance: fear their masters! It was then, after thinking on this, that the Scientists and Geneticists, who preceded their ancestors to this planet, decided that the next thing they should do was to experiment on some of the human slaves and islanders! They decided to use human DNA, along with mixing animal or reptilian DNA, or both; plus, the DNA from one of the full blooded 'gods', the Annunaki, who were the Kings there, mixing it with the DNA of whatever creature they would be altering! Some of the Scientists and Geneticists went to neighboring islands, taking several city slaves with them. These were slaves who knew the Islands well. The Geneticists selected their specimens: animal, bird, insect, reptile and human! It is from these experiments creatures such as the giant Cyclopes, with the large eye in the center of the forehead; the Unicorn; the Pegasus; and the Satyr; among others, came to be! Many are today the characters you have read or heard about in stories, legends and myths; and also, in Sci-Fi and Fantasy books! Whatever the Scientists, the Geneticists, and the Rulers, could conceive to be, they attempted to create! And it is from their experiments that I came to be! Yes, I too was an experiment of the Atlantian-Annunaki giant 'gods' from another planet!

After many years of perfecting their experimental alterations on animal, reptilian, bird, and other smaller species; such as insects; they then succeeded in creating the huge reptilian-bird-like creature I know as: me, I, and sometimes, **why**? Yes, I eventually had begun wondering **why** I was created. What purpose had it brought? What good would my existing be, not just to the world but to me? *Why* was I to be alone? *Why* create a something with no real thought, neither of its purpose, nor of its feelings and existence, leaving it to perhaps know only fear and agony? **Why? Why?** So I became more of a Why than an I...

The addition of the Annunaki's DNA made whatever they created much larger than the original species they began with. This was because the Aliens, the Watchers/Nephilim-fallen Angels/Annunaki, who came from the sky, were not originally from this Earth; and so in Earth's standards, those who came from the sky, who also created the city of Atlantis, populated it, and then populated other islands across the ocean, was considered giants! The Atlantians of the Nephilim unadulterated, pure blood, from the sky, rose to the heights of eighteen to over thirty feet tall! Their breeding with humans produced off-springs that stood anywhere from seven feet to eighteen feet tall. These were said to be the Annunaki. When the giant's half hybrid human off-springs bred with a human as well, they usually produced off springs that were six feet or less... but sometimes taller. Yes, Atlantis was a city of what was referred to then as the home of the giants or gods and demi-gods! It therefore, was a city of Alien Giants from the stars! But there, living in that city, were also their half human and half god mixed children, plus their off-springs, children who had even lesser 'god' DNA. They all lived there with the full blooded 'gods'; and all were loved by them. This size difference meant there were various heights of buildings, and people in the city of Atlantis. These people came forth from the off springs of the more advanced Atlantian people living on Earth at the time, with the Annunaki. Others were the results of alterations on the ape-like people here at that time, then the mating of them with the Annunaki. This was why there were smaller buildings and extremely tall ones that seemed to reach to the heavens; and why and how their door framed pillars were created much larger than people are today. The twenty-plus foot tall columns/pillars were made with polished white minerals; some were granite with a composition of quartz crystals, which made them heavy, far too heavy for any man of today to lift without machinery. Since it is believed there was not the technology in that time period capable of making the pillars, nor erecting such huge and heavy columns; those of today, are still amazed and wonder how they were carried and lifted to make these structures and statues. For there was indeed also large life-size stone statues sculptured in the images of those who earned remembrance. These Annunaki who came from the other world from the sky, on their planet could live for over a thousand plus years, for their planet rotated at a slower speed than Earth's. Here on Earth their life span was shortened, but still, those who had only the 'god's' blood, lived to be close to, or well over a thousand years, if they remained on this planet. Their off-springs, those with human blood, lived for four to eight hundred years; and some even a bit longer. So they had plenty of time to re-create this world and its life forms.

I, the Phoenix, was created from several of the creation here on this planet, which they, the Nephilim, the Annunaki- Atlantians, and their helpers: the Reptilian race, and the Sirians, had captured and then combined to produce me. They first took a huge lizard and combined its DNA with a huge ancient bird-like creature. You today would call these huge creatures' dinosaurs. Yes, there were dinosaurs here when they first came, and there were dinosaurs here when I was being created. They even created some of the dinosaurs. The giants from the stars had captured some of these dinosaurs, such as the tall, docile, long necked herbivores, and the stalky hard armored ones, and used them to haul stones and trees; heavy metals; and machinery; plus, whatever else they needed hauled! Since these long necks could swim, it not only was a plus for the Atlantians, but it also made it easier for them to haul heavy or multiple things all at once, to and from that great city of Atlantis! To create my parents, the Atlantian-Nephilim-Annunaki Geneticists and Scientists, had experimented at first on three main creatures: the lizard; the bird-like creature that stood on two long legs and had a long and pointy beak, which you of today call the heron; and a giant bat creature. The Nephilim and Annunaki Geneticists added a small amount of something they had created in their labs and fed to their vegetables and fruit plants. They fed my parents and later myself, plus the other creatures they were experimenting upon, with the manna: the food of the 'gods', which was a powerfully nutritious and highly oxidized algae from the plant family! It is the first plant life to grow on this planet. The algae could make, whenever they applied it in a certain sequence, whatever they were creating grow very large and tall. The results of this combination of species created what your Earth history calls a flying dinosaur: the Pterodactyl! This alien Nephilim-Annunaki giant race of people created many of the dinosaurs! The remains of the dinosaurs discovered by humans many years after their disappearance were established to date back over thousands of years. There are a small percentage of the dinosaurs still existing on Earth, mostly undetected, the rest vanishing with Atlantis. However, the algae were not the only thing that allowed life to grow to gigantic proportions, compared to the height of things today. The algae only permitted things to grow to whatever its full potential would allow. It kept things supplied with the oxygen and nutrient they required. You see, back during those times, there was a canopy that covered the entire planet! This Canopy allowed the right moisture, right air pressure, light, and oxygen levels, both for plant and all other species under the canopy. The planet then, had a higher air pressure than you have today. This air pressure contributed to the gigantic growths of all creation: plant, mammal, insect, water life, reptiles and minerals, and etc. An interesting thing happens when things become greatly enlarged. The life here that is deadly to you, such as poisonous snakes and insects, were not poisonous then, when they were of gigantic proportion; and if all were to return back to the canopy filament the Earth once had, your poisonous species of today would lose their poisonous venom and produce healing venom instead! This was the blessing and beauty of the Eco system then. So with the help of the canopy's air pressure and the food of the 'gods', my parents grew, and I grew, quickly, from the smaller size that we were when first created! Some creatures then were already giants when the spiritually falling ones, the Aliens: the Nephilim arrived here on Earth! These of course became the Annunaki and Atlantians in mass body form, instead of ethereal; now also the ancestors of those beings that came from another world!

With the Pterodactyl, they continued experimenting, altering its DNA; even inserting selective chromosomes and codes from it, and from their own, to combine and enhance the creature's capability to understand words and make decisions. A very dangerous and risky gift to give to such a creature as from it I became! So arrogant were they, due to their great delight in creating, that they did not properly, nor completely, consider all the possibilities of harm they could be creating! They believed they had a right to create and destroy, with a clear conscious, for they believed if they created a something, they then had the right and the permission to un-create it; no laws broken, not even a sacred one… so they believed…

They had eventually decided to insert small crystals of various colors and kinds inside of me. This was to be their final application of completing me. Some of these crystals vibrated at a speed faster than light, such as the quartz crystal. It vibrates at 786,000 pulses per millisecond, moving faster than light! These stones were to create a powerful energy and communicative means for the Scientists and Geneticists to use to try and control us! Some of these stones they had lined all the way up my parent's and my spine; embedding them in our organs and brain! When I was hatched, and but only eight weeks old, they had tricked and temporary captured my parents so they could steal me from my nest! They took me to their lab and there they inserted the multicolored crystals into me in the same places and arrangement they did with both my parents! Again, a very daring and risky thing to do, giving power to a new creation they did not yet know nor understand! They continued on with their many alterations on all three of us. With me, they also added the DNA of an insect, known today as the ant. They had now combined within me, but not my parents, the DNA of a plant; an insect; a mammal; a bird; and a reptile! We were constantly being altered! We were weary of this and becoming angry, hating them; greatly longing to escape and find freedom and a safe place…a place of our own to live out our days and raise our future young! But they kept close eyes upon us, both by the frightened slaves who came to deliver food and water with a long handled scoop, and by their powerful spying mechanical flying camera scopes, and drones that could zoom in on us, whether we were on land or in the sky of our clear domed caged enclosure!

They had created first my parents, and then they proceeded to changing me from what my parents had brought forth in the egg; the egg my mother long and lovingly protected; keeping warm day and night so I could be! Those Scientists and Geneticists had changed me; wanting to re-create even what they had created! They wanted to create a new me, different from my parents! And, **why** did they create me and my parents? Because they could! They had gotten so caught up in their successes that it blinded them to what they did! When they had created my parents before me, who mated and hatched me, and then saw us becoming more majestic and powerful with every alteration, they wanted to keep improving upon us; see what betterment they could make out of us! They had also noticed a light in our eyes that spoke of intelligence and understanding, so this excited them, motivating them to expand upon it…upon us! But then they began to notice something else in our eyes of intelligence! They saw the hate and the anger! They now finally realized what they may have created! They then began to concern themselves that we could be a threat to them, rather than us being their slaves, and *them* our masters! This is why they had decided to insert crystals and various stones inside us! They thought they could use the crystals and stones as a device of communication and control! But what they did not consider, at least not very seriously, was that if the crystals were embedded in us then they, the crystals, and we, could become one, thus, be capable of using them for **our** benefit, and **not** giving the Atlantians power over us! And that is what we eventually did! The Geneticists and Scientists' plan was that by lining the crystals up in a certain sequence it would provide activation of the DNA coding within us that engages and activates the more serene Spirit of the brain and the Soul. This would 'tame' us should we show aggressiveness that could lead to danger towards them or even us! They also experimented with special wave tones and patterns of sound, light, and color. They applied stimulating words, frequencies, and tones; plus symbolic designs; all to gain control over the hostile section of our brains! It was obvious they received a great enjoyment, excitement, and feeling of power from what they did, and had been doing, and also from their thinking that they could create new life, even a powerful creature, such as my family which they believed they could control and master! I was but still a hatchling, but they were intelligent enough to recognize the light of knowing, understanding, and intelligence that they saw in my eyes looking at back at them... and especially the other thing they saw in my eyes...

My eyes would be gentle as they first looked within them, and then they would change, almost slowly, almost quickly; becoming intensified, more pronounced, and at times, more sequenced; staring them down with a hint of confidence, anger and hate! Yes, I was but a young one, barely experiencing life, yet those who were experimenting on us were smart enough, and had lived long enough, hundreds of years, to recognize what they saw staring back at them! I, even at that young infant age, began to know the feel of power! And indeed it was additive! I was me, a new and innocent being, yet I was also them, carrying within me *their* DNA! Carrying all their instinctive and inherited nature! It was then I saw their first fear and regret; their first beginning of doubting that they would ever have control over me! It may not have lasted very long, their emotions I saw, but I had seen them, and what's more, I had *felt* them! Yes indeed, power had a 'delicious taste' and feel! It had additive, and self-preservation power! And, I would use *all* the power I'd gain that they'd given to me to one day free my parents, and myself, from this captivity, and from the painful and cruel experiments that were continuously done on us!

I remember the day I was hatched. I was finally born! I was born from a father and mother who had finally been successfully created after many years of experimental failures; being altered over and over again to create what the Scientists and Geneticists felt was the perfection of what they had first altered! After the Scientists and Geneticists were satisfied in their creation of my parents, my parents were then taken to an isolated nearby island and tied by one leg with a chain of some strong metal substance. The chains were secured to two different large, thick trees. Their flying was limited to the length of the metal chain attached to their leg. It allowed them to fly and walk nine times their length, but never close enough for them to touch one another. Water could be reached, for a lake was near them. Game could be caught, at times, should it venture too close; but mostly the food was brought to them by the slaves of the city, or the islanders nearby. My mother and father had spent many months just beyond each other's reach before they were encouraged to mate and produce me. I remember my loving parents well, even to this day, tens of thousands of years later! Memory lasts longer in those who can live for so many years as I. This I am grateful for, because then I can smile when I think upon Atlantis, because they there gave to me my parents whom I love deeply; and they gave me the start of what I later became, and what, and who I am today.

My parents at times glowed from the many tiny crystals embedded in them. I loved their gentle glow, and soon learned to recognized them first by their glow, and then by their smell! I was hatched from a large green, purple speckled, and scaly, rock-like egg, which my Dear mother protected day and night; never leaving her nest where I bedded! My father at that time, would hunt for her, flying up to her, delivering his kill, when he could chance upon it; and also delivered the food and water the slaves left for us. My father kept careful watch over us, day and night, both of them excited about the time I would be hatched…their first born! After I was hatched he would continue hunting and gathering food for my mother, and now also for me, until I was trained and capable of doing it for myself.

 My mother was larger than my father. She was twenty-five feet long from a raised beak to extended toes! Her wing span, from the longest tip of one wing across to the other, was over sixty feet! My father was ten feet smaller in wing and body; and I? I grew to be fifteen feet larger than even my mother!

The day I'd hatched I was just beginning to be. I'd been pecking throughout most the night. My mother and father watched excited! The Scientists had small flying machines that contained a camera that could record scenes and sound, sending them back to them in the city; so they too were watching. You of today call those small, round, spying machines: drones. The Scientists, Geneticists, Rulers, and other important officials, were taking turns watching us throughout the night. Then when the sun began to rise, and darkness still with it, I emerged, breaking free at last to greet the re-birth of the new day! I let out a loud screech, and my parents, happily fussed over me. The dark olive green, purple speckled egg I came from was ten feet long and oval shaped. It stayed this color up until the last hour, of the very day I was hatched! That's when it began to pulse with light, and produce iridescent multi-colors, extending outward from the shell. When I broke free of it, multi-colors also emerged with me, growing brighter and more shimmering, extending thirteen feet above and around me, for thirty seconds or more! Its light was casting a rainbow glow upward, and around my parents as well! I can imagine the expressions on the faces of those who observed us. They were probably filled with shock, awe, and surprise; then joy, and a huge ego expansion, at what *'they'* had created; 'patting their own backs', giving **themselves** *all the* credit!

We were permitted to continue living where we nested, but the day I was to test out my leathery bat-like wings was the day they limited, yet planned to extend, our freedom as well! They had put up a clear domed barrier and cut my parent's chains, just before they mated and I was formed in an egg. They had created a dome at that time, sending only slaves to our island with long handled metal cutters to cut the chains around my parent's legs. They were to do this in hopes that my parents would mate and be successful in producing a fertile egg. Before I was hatched they had come, and with much difficulty, and a long time spent, replaced the chains around my parent's ankles, but only allowing just enough length for them to fly to the nest, and never allowing my father to reach further than the one edge of the nest! Therefore they could never reach one another! Why they did this I do not know for it made no sense to me! Then when I was six weeks old they returned to remove the chains and extend the doom to over twice its original size. Instead of sending only the slaves as they had done when they had first cut the chains, the Atlantians, anxious to see me, had accompanied, this day, their slaves to our island. Ha! I laugh a little each time I think upon that day, or at least the happier part of that day, for it was a day that made us feel more powerful then they! It was also comical to us because of how they acted in their fear of us! They were afraid of us, that was obvious by the manner in which they tried to remove my parent's chains! Oh how I smile when I envision that moment! There my parents and I were, on the ground, beneath our nest. We stood quite still, seeming calm and harmless, but watching every movement the slaves, Geneticists, and Scientists made! The Scientists were instructing the slaves on what to do, but they stood much further away from us than did their slaves! The Geneticists and Scientists stayed close to their hoover craft, standing inside them, readying to fly with the first indication of danger! These hover-crafts where made for them to sit or stand up on. They had clear round dome casings made of a very strong and unpenetrable material. The crafts could hover to the sides and up or down! All of them were outside of the doom. One of the Scientists held a remote in his hand. This remote could raise a section, like a door of the dome we were enclosed in, and lower it. They wanted to raise it slightly, but be large enough for the slaves to lie down upon their abdomens and push the metal cutters through to cut the chains off of my parent's ankles. The Atlantians remember, were very tall, and the slaves were short, around five feet and less. Because of that the Atlantians could raise the dome a shorter distance up, allowing their slaves to lie on their abdomens, pushing the metal staff/cutters through and enabling control of the cutters without the dome being raise high enough for me to escape. I wasn't chained so they did not want to chance my escaping. When they went to cut the chains they were attempting to cut not the ring around the ankles, but rather, the link three feet away from my parent's ankles, due to their fear of my parents; and I believe, even me! For some reason I found even this humorous! As the metal staff cutter neared my parents, they slowly lowered their heads, watching the staff, amused! I knew they were amused because, after all, I am one of them, and, as you would say in a cliché: 'a chip off of the old block!' I remember the staff moving slowly towards them, almost sneaky-like, as if they thought they could fool us, and we'd be too unintelligent to know what it was and what they and it were trying to do! I suppose the Scientists never told them we were most likely smarter than them, the slaves! It all soon took upon a game-like quality for my parents! My parents next, slowly lifted their massive heads and played Stupid! They even gave their heads a wobbly-bop for affect, and their eyes a bit of a roll around! I had to try hard to stifle a squawky-chuckle! I almost let it out, but did not want to spoil the fun of the game! The slaves seeing my parent's actions, thinking them uninterested and stupid, were encouraged to advance the cutting staff. The Scientists watching, I believe, began to suspect that my parents were up to something, either that, or my parents were having convulsions! The Scientists' eyes began to widen a bit at first, then narrowed in their wonderment and suspension of what they were seeing! My parents allowed the slaves to move their metal cutting staffs closer as they began pattering their chained foot, and the unchained one, in little unbalanced movements, while bobbing their heads up and down and from side to side, while rolling their eyes! They even opened their beaks to take on the look of delirium! The expressions on the Geneticists and Scientists' faces, along with the expressions of concentration and confidence on the slaves' faces; and them sprawled out on their bellies, creeping the metal staffs closer to my parents, while my parents put on their mindless act, all came together to me as the funniest thing I could imagined! Of course, I was very young then, and this was the first experience I'd had that 'tickled my funny bone! Still, to this day, I find *that* part funny, even after all these thousands of years! The Scientists' display of slight fear that caused them to stay close or inside their hovering crafts, to me was humorous! Oh the ironic nature of it! They had believed and acted as if **they** had *all* the power! They had created us with the intent to master and over power **us**, and here *they* were afraid of *us*! It just seemed comical to me that they were the ones who were afraid; afraid of what they had created to be over-powered, mastered, and deemed weaker than them! *'Play with 'fire' and you risk the possibility of being 'burn by fire!'* I had said to them in my thoughts!

꧁꧂꧁꧂꧁꧂꧁꧂꧁꧂꧁꧂꧁꧂

My parents must have thought the same thing, for I heard their thoughts saying to them: '*We will give you an example of what you **might have** created, or **have** created! And what many possibilities, good and not so good, might become of it, aimed for you and your kind; foolish, foolish people!*' My parents kept up their act, always with one eye upon the metal cutting staff. They were still doing their strange "dance". Then, just as the staff was about to cut the chain attached to my mother's foot, about three feet from her ankle; and at the same time the other staff was ready to bare down and cut my father's chain, that was also three feet or so from his ankle, my parents signaled to one another with their eyes and thoughts, and then let out this loud screech, flapping their huge wings, and jumping forward to grab the metal cutting staffs, lifting the staffs and the slaves along with them into the air, and then away from them! The slaves, as well as the Scientists, were startled by this and jumped! The two slaves that were lying on their stomachs, pushing the metal staff cutters, were pulled inside the dome when my parents had, at a quick speed, grabbed up the staffs to sling them away! Terrified, the native slaves quickly headed back for the opening, trying to scamper through in fear that we would tear them apart! They had been dragged quickly through the opening of the dome, losing their grip on the staffs, unfortunate for them; and were now in reach of my parents! I wasn't chained, and had decided to join in this game of my parents! I flapped my small wings, gave out a loud squawk; bent my head, with my beak open; and then I spread wide my wings, charging for the two terrified, scampering slaves! They were so frightened that they did not at first, take the time to get up and run! I allowed them to manage that by slowing down. I have to admit, it was a great feeling, that feeling that 'little' baby me could frighten these grown men! I had, just before my actions, quickly figured out what my parents were doing! Their intentions were not to harm anyone, only mock them, and have fun doing it! They were making fun of the Scientists and Geneticists, who thought they were so superior to us; who thought *they* were the intelligent ones, and *we*, 'some dumb creatures' beneath them in *all* *ways*! Ha! Little did they know then what they had created, and what they had helped bring forth from those creations by their mixing our DNA with those other life forms, and, with their own, preparing what was yet to become: ME!

Aw, but back to my story…My parents were smiling, so proud of me! If you could have seen the slaves, Geneticists, and Scientists' faces, and how the slaves struggled to get under the dome and away from us; while the Scientists began to, in their own panic, quickly push the button to lowered the dome, you would have thought it all harmless and comical as well! But it was not as harmless as it seemed. You see, there was a section of the dome that served as a door, and it was this section that had been raised so the slaves could get the metal staff cutters under, yet not high enough for me to get under and out! But in the Scientists' panic they feared I would rush the slaves, get out and away, or come for them! That was when the fun ended… No, not because the slaves got outside the dome safely, and the dome lowered, but because the Scientists had selfishly, in their fright, lowered the dome door *before* the slaves could get **completely** out! We had meant no harm, only having fun, yet these so called smart Scientists had reacted without clear thought in their actions due to a greater concern for *themselves;* not considering the slave's safety! The dome came down quickly, cutting off the legs of one of the slaves and cutting in half the other one! Their screams were terrible! We were shocked at these people's actions and lack of regard for others! I stopped immediately when this happened; my fun turned to disbelief, and a bit confused! I slowly turned to look at my parents. They too had stopped smiling, their enjoyment abruptly ended! My mother motioned for me to come under her wing. I turned and wobbled to her side, gladly going under her large, warm, and comforting wing. *'Why did they hurt them?' I asked.* My mother looked at my father, and him, her. I suppose they did not want me to feel it was my fault. Finally my father spoke. *'They had not intended to. The dome door came down too quickly'.* I looked at him then up at my mother. She nodded her head. I then looked at the human body parts that where left inside our domed home. My father spoke, *'We will not touch them, but let them be a reminder of how arrogance and fear can cripple one in many ways. Let this be a teacher for you daughter, that as you grow and know your own power, you will not allow selfishness, greed, fear, and arrogance to rule you; and you will think your plans through carefully!* **We** *did not, and so this is another lesson for us!'* Then he slowly turned his head to the body parts left behind in our domed home: two legs of the one slave, and the legs and lower torso of the other; all still jerking! My mother and I also turned to sadly look at them as well. There was a lot of blood, and although it looked and smelled like food, we looked and thought of it as poison! I glanced up at those on the other side, several Scientists and Geneticists, plus several much shorter and fearful slaves. The slaves were looking at their mutated friends with disbelief and shocked expressions! But the Scientists were watching *us*! Several of the slaves had moved quickly to the unconscious, but still alive, crippled slave with the severed legs. They lifted and carried him over to the Scientists. The Scientists had the slaves tie off the injured, unconscious slave's leg stubs with some cord to stop any more of the blood from bleeding out! Then they had the slaves carry, and lift him into one of their hoover crafts to be taken to the city for the healers to try and save him; for the Healers not only had medicinal herbs, but also laser and other technology for healing. The Scientists left in their hoover crafts, while the other slaves sadly walked to their canoes, heading back to Atlantis. The slaves were talking nervously to one another, looking back at us and the remains of their friends! We watched them go, realizing we may have cheated ourselves of our freedom…

It was about three days later that they came back with their hoover crafts, slaves, and long metal chain cutters. They looked a bit surprised to see we had not touched the rotting body parts that were stinking up our concealed home. The heat was rotting them quickly and the blow flies and other insects were feasting and laying their eggs in the rotting flesh. It reminded us of how great intelligence can soon turn to fear, stupidly, harm, and arrogance…*and*… isolation…

The body parts were retrieved three days after they were left there inside our closed dome. They would be burnt or toss to the sea! When the bodies were removed, so were my parent's chains. Yes, we had *not* challenged them in any way this time. Not just so my parents could be *finally* free to fly without chains, but because we did not wish to unintentionally cause any more harm. These Atlantians were unpredictable! We learned later that the Scientists had immediately gone back to their labs and worked alongside of the Engineers and Metallurgists to create the laser that would set us free! This laser was the strange beam that was soon directed towards my parent's chains! The islander slaves had used this laser beam to cut the ring the chain was **directly** attached to, around their ankles. Fortunately my parents sensed there could be danger with this new instrument because the Scientists were smart enough to use, as a warning, the laser beam on a section of the chain that was further away from their leg. I now believe that they did this because they realized, at the moment when they had been staring at us, the day of the accident, and just before they had departed, that we were *more* intelligent then they gave us credit for; that we were very *aware* of what we were doing! So they now believed we were intelligent enough to understand their motives, and decided to show us what their new instrument could do by cutting through the hard metal with their new laser beam, slicing the chains in two, as if the metal was made of butter! We saw its power; and it was easy to realize what possible harm it could do, so we stood quite still… even me. I did not want the beam to slip and cut through my parent's leg, so I did not move nor make a sound. We understood well the message they were sending us about what their new cutting tool could do to us if we moved! We were simply satisfied, content, and grateful, that they had returned and *still* wanted to set us free to fly and move about in the dome, unrestricted by heavy chains! This new cutting tool of theirs provided them safety and us a quicker and freer release! Freer cause there would be no heavy, dangling chains attached to my parent's legs, as there would have been if the metal staff cutters had been used! So, it turned out, that both we and the Scientists gained from its invention...and sadly from the accident...

The Atlantis Scientists continued practicing controlling us, especially me, since they felt that starting with me right away, while I was but an infant, would ensure greater and quicker control! They began trying to controlling us with sound. They tried to produce those sounds they found successful with their own voices, vibrating in their throats, while using a device attached around their necks and close to the larynx. They had some success, and the sounds were ways for us to communicate with them as well. Let them think they were mastering us, we said to ourselves, for we knew the reasons we allowed their sound system to work! But we allowed it to work only so far; *never* to **control us!** After a time, they tried using certain word commands. They wanted to domesticate us! We were to be their pets, and their 'guard dogs'! They wanted us to protect them and their city! We were not perfected for that, especially my parents.

The area inside the dome, which they had later again enlarged, concealing us in, was a much larger area than the one before. This one was ten times its size! It was five miles wide by five miles long, and two hundred feet high! Inside this area there were large beds of clear water; and there were enclosed and living there, many animals for us to feast upon; but there were also people living there, captured by the dome; people, not of the god-blood of the Atlantian Kings and Queens which had come from the sky! These people were the native islanders!

When after a time, the larger animals became scarce, from our hunting and devouring them, and leaving only the smaller ones, we had to then kill more in number and more often because of their much smaller size. This then greatly affected the population, and therefore, **everyone's** food supply! Our food source began to dwindle down to nothing...We began to starve… We were so hungry, growing thin and desperate. The never ending hunger kept us awake; the pain in our bellies, eating at our insides, and the driving hunger force, was driving us to uncontrollable desperation to fill up with anything that would stop the pain and still the master of our insides that was beginning to control us, forcing us to do what we did next…

The Atlantians no longer came bringing us food. We were on our own. My parents were very concerned for my life, and would dive for what few fish were left in the waters, and feed these to me, taking only a small portion for them, many times regurgitating even that for me to eat. We turned to berries, nuts and seeds; to reptiles, insects, and worms, for our nourishment in order to survive. We saw the Atlantian's drones flying over and along the sides of our dome, so we knew that they knew we were starving. Was this their way of destroying us; of saying *they* were the masters, and held the power, not us? Were they punishing us? I was very young, but I had grown fast, so I required more food then we could find… So it was only predictable that we did the only thing left to do. Our survival instincts were on high drive, kicked in at top speed; our hunger ruling us, 'kicking' us into action to do what we would not have done *if* all these elements of forces did not *now* control us!: we began hunting the humans!

First, with great control, and there was little of it left, we killed and ate their food source, and then they too began to starve! They had raised and harvested pigs, fowls, dogs, sheep, horses, grains, vegetables, roots, fruit, berries, and nuts. It was not enough! The Islanders, the humans, were of course very frightened of us. We were huge, many times their size, over five times their height! They would blow their breath into large spiraling sea shells as a warning when those on watch saw us coming, flying towards their villages! They would then grab the children up into their arms and run to their huts, barring the doors, praying for protection! The men would crouch behind structures made of wood, stone, and straw, holding bows with arrows, and long, sharp, spears that had pointy sharpened flint, or obsidian stones, on the ends! They also had blow-darts for their defense against any threats to them. *We* now were their threat; and we came hard and fast! We knew we had to control our new master, called hunger, inside, and not take more than we needed to keep us for a day. But it was proving more and more difficult to remain in control over this new master! When we flew over head the sun was blocked out, so large were we! The people who survived later told stories of how the sun fled, least it be eaten by us as well! We, at first, took only the smallest of anything warm blooded, other than the humans, so that our food source would last longer. When all of the human's food sources were expired, and the fishes in the waters gone as well, the only other thing left to eat was: the humans! We could smell their warm, hot blood pumping in their veins, calling us to sacrifice the flesh it was in! Yet, we hesitated, our hunger not yet reaching again that insane push to consume, consume, consume! Still, the Atlantians did not rescue us, nor the humans! They did not seem to care, not only not for us, their hard to achieve control over products of their creation, but also they seemed to not care about the humans who lived here! *That,* we found lower than human, dangerous, senseless, and evil! And here we were, the ones who were *not* human nor gods, appearing to be the dangerous, evil, and lower species, and yet, it was **we** who were humane and merciful in our thoughts and intentions! Evil truly was in the eyes of the beholder...

The tiny crystal implants of various colors and frequencies which the Scientists had embedded in our heads, nervous system, organs, and along our spine to activate the body through the Soul for serenity, so to help better control us, was canceled out by the body's need to survive; and so it should have been expected what we did next. Why those who were intelligent enough to create us did not foresee what happened, or even when they saw through their cameras that our food source was running out, why they did not do something to ensure the safety of the natives, and ensure that we had either more game to kill or food brought to us so we would not turn to the eating of the humans, did not make sense, even to us, unless…unless they were *again* experimenting with us! My parents acted on natural instincts of preservation for themselves, and for their starving child: **me!** Yes, we fed on human flesh! I did not kill the humans, but my parents did. Something inside of me had held me back, but even I, when presented with the regurgitated flesh, ate it, for I was so **very** hungry! It turned out this was another of the Scientists' experiments to see what we would do, and how well their crystal control system worked on us!

After the first kill and feed we'd made on the native's flesh, the Scientists seemed to decide to stop their experiment. They had moved our domed barrier to another area of the island. Fortunately for us, it was an island that stretched out to cover over a thirty mile span! We now again had more game for food, *minus* the humans! When they had shifted the dome cage, we were moved along with it. Their technology was such that they only had to raise the dome a few feet up from the bottom before a clear dome bottom extended across. We were then lifted above the tree lines and deposited a few miles from, and in between, the native's villages. The natives there were safe and we were saved! This is how I came to be, and how I was raised; but I need to tell you that it was *not* the Atlantian Scientists and Geneticists who had the last 'hand' in creating me, the Phoenix…

After a time they loss all control over me, for a higher and Supreme Essence began to take guardianship over me! I, much later, learned it was the Divine of the Pure Light, of the All of all creation that took back its control of creation! The Scientists and Geneticists had begun the alterations that created the form I was, but the Divine found in me a higher purpose, and so took me away from Atlantis, and created what I am today…

Over the years I had come to know and love the people of that city on the sea. The children would wave to me, laugh and toss up to me morsels of meat. How could they do this if I was encased in a dome, away from the city? I shall tell you… After the Scientists, Geneticists, and Rulers of the city saw that I was thriving well, and that my parents and I were docile and sound of mind, they decided to separate me from my parents, releasing them to the wild… After they released my parents from me they moved the dome barrier I was in, when and wherever they liked! That wherever sometimes included over their city! They felt safe in doing this because they also had a dome covering their city. This was an unbreakable strong clear dome which they could erect over their city, and open as wide as they desired! And close or open, as quickly as needed! They even had another dome of hard metal that they could rise to cover that! That second dome was made of a hard unknown metal from another world, that was so hard, nothing known on Earth, and not created by them, could break through! Yes, they had begun to trust that I would not harm them, and they trusted that they could use their high technology to stop me should they be wrong. This meant they would be present outside when I was moved over their city, and that my visits there were time limited! I was happy to have the changes in scenery, and soon developed fondness and an appreciation for the children and the sights of the sparkling copper, bronze, gold and white city. But even this was not enough to still the grief and loneliness that accompanied the loss of my parents…When my parents were released; I was not allowed to follow! It was a trick the Scientists had pulled upon us to succeed in releasing my parents, yet keeping me contained! My parents had been napping; I happily and contended underneath the warm protection of my mother's wing; my father lying beside my mother and I in our large nest; their heads resting on one another's neck, happy and contended also. We had adapted to our environment and way of surviving. I was at that time, six months old in human's Earth's time, but six years old according to our DNA structure. I was still considered more of an infant in my species development, like most species of Earth, other than the human race; and I was still in much need of the love and company of my parents! The separation was staged when the Scientists had sent a bee-like small drone. They had sent it closer to the side of our dome than they ever had any other drone in the pass. They had it move quickly back and forth, but only inches, like as if it was vibrating like a giant bee! Then they would move it, like a bee, first closer to us, high up in the tree outside the dome, but where we had our nest. Then it would quickly move away! Somehow they had even managed to have it tap the dome gently, producing a soft sound that did not awaken me, but sent an instinctive protective alert to my protective parents! Because the drone moved so strangely, and was new to them, my parents wanted to observe it to be certain that it could not penetrate the dome and inflict harm to me or to them. I did not awake, so deep into contended sleep was I. My loving parents looked up and around at this strange tapping something, and then they carefully, my father first, rose up to get a better look. The Scientists, we soon found out, could also slide back the top of the dome. Oh they seemed to have thought of everything when they made our cage! The dome's top was quickly opened and the drone came towards my father then pulled away. Father moved out of the dome, concentrating on the mysterious something, concerned for our safety! Doing this he had not, at that moment, realized he was outside the dome! My mother saw him go towards the drone, and the drone move towards him! She immediately rose up to fight for her mate and for her child, even to the death, if it became necessary! In her haste, focused on her intentions and the sight before her, she too exited the dome! At that moment the dome slid rapidly closed, within mere moments; causing my parents to look back, now realizing they were no longer within the closure of the dome! But their thoughts were not happy, nor on their at long last, freedom to go where ever they choice, and as high up as they had dreamed of! No, it was full of panic and desperation to get back *inside* to their sleeping child! They began pecking on the dome, increasing the strength of force to try and penetrate it! I heard the pecking and opened my eyes! I then raised my head, soon realizing my parents were no longer lying next to me. I glanced up towards the sound of the loud continuous pecking to see both my parents ***outside*** the dome trying to get ***inside!*** I was confused at first. So many questions entered my mind. *'How did they get outside? Why were they so panicked and sad looking?'* These were some of the many questions that went through my mind so rapidly that it gave me confusion! My parents were looking at me, emitting a deep and terrible sadness and concern! I stood up in my nest watching them, raising my wings slightly to stretch them. They began to squawk, communicating to me that *they loved me and would find a way back inside to be with me; for me to not be afraid!* They told me what had happened. That is how I knew and was able to share this with you. My parents tried so hard. They even faced the drone, now realizing it was a camera, and pleaded with the Scientists! My parents, of course, knew the Scientists did not understand our language, but they hoped they would understand their expressions and actions and show compassion for us; releasing either me, to be with them, or open the dome and allow them to go back inside to be with me! But the Scientists revealed no compassion, no concern; only indifference; cold, hard, indifference! I cried out to my parents, becoming as sad and desperate to be with them as they were to be with me! I flew up to the top of the dome where they were on the opposite side! They had not meant to frighten me, only to let me know that they had not deliberately left me behind; and for me to have faith that all would turn out well. Oh how we wanted to believe that! We tried for hours to break open the dome! But even as big and strong as we were, no matter how long and how hard we tried, the dome and the Atlantians would not yield; and we could not penetrate on our own, the barrier between us! We were exhausted; sore of throat, beak, and wing, from crying out and beating our wings and beaks against the hard and solid dome! We had expended all the energy we had. We tried to be calm and have faith that there was a humane characteristic infused within the Atlantians that would, and could, empathize with the feelings of a parent towards their child, and a young child's needs; plus the child's sorrowful and terrified feelings of losing her parents…but they did not; they cared not…

I could not last as long as my parents, for they were stronger than me! I had to save enough energy to fly back down to my nest. I flew to my nest hours before my parents had to fly to a tree to restore their energy so to be able to try perhaps another tactic. My once cozy nest now felt so strangely cold and empty…lonely…so very lonely… My parents were highly intelligent, but they had their limitations. They tried so hard, truly they did! I began to cry, perhaps not like you cry, but still I was crying; and if I had the ability to shed tears of sorrow they would have poured almost continuously, for I was truly in deep sorrow. All parts of me cried out for the warmth, comfort, love and company of my Dear parents! I cried also for them, feeling their sorrow and knowing they also cried for me, and even for themselves… My parents rested and then flew to the ground to hopefully find a weak spot at the bottom of the dome. They remembered the door-like section that had been raised up for the slaves, month's back, so perhaps there would be a tiny sliver of an open space they could insert the pointy part of their beak into and succeed in raising a portion of the dome so they could get to me. Oh how it hurt my soul, and *still* does, when I remember back to that time; even after these tens of thousands of years later! It hurt so deeply, not only because I thought I might never get to be with my loving parents again, but also it hurt me deeply to see how deeply, desperately, and frantically, they had tried to get to me; harming themselves in the process! I, and my parents: creatures thought to be void of affection, reasoning, and compassion, among other attributes, felt what apparently, the Atlantians in power did not, and perhaps could not; for we felt those feelings and attributes! We felt all the emotions of what was happening! And, those emotions were 'killing us', in their own way; slowly and ceaselessly…

My parents stayed close, but they had to hunt to survive. They would make short trips away and thoughtfully ate not in front of me, but ate where they found their meal. I was forced, by the cruel actions of those who had released my parents, to hunt for myself. I had been taught by my parents to learn by observing them when they hunted. They even had allowed me, on several occasions, to hunt and kill my own small game! Many years later, when I was fully grown, I figured those who had separated us must have saw that I could successfully hunt and capture the smaller game; and so they had made sure the dome was over a place with lots of small game. I had to learn fast if I were to survive! My parents were proud of how quickly I learned; and were comforted by this, for they knew I would not starve as they had first feared. My parents, and I, never did break through the dome; nor did we find a way to get it to yield for us. My parents stayed for as long as the nature of all creatures, besides humans, would permit. The driving cycle of nature was beginning to take over my parents. For us it apparently 'hit' the adults when a child turned twelve years old, more, or a little less. That meant they stayed for six more months of Earth's time outside the dome to be with me. For me it was nowhere near long enough; but that was when they flew away from me, and towards the call of the wild… It propelled them naturally, so they could no longer stay. We were not like the other non-human, or so called gods, that lived on the earth at that time. But we could think, plan, and intuit. So, my parents sensed the change ahead of time coming upon them; and before it took *all* control of them they told me what was about to occur. They told me that I had come of the age where nature considered me grown and capable, necessary so, to be released to mature further on my own; to learn about life; how to survive on my own, and then one day find a mate and birth children of my own! They said, with sorrow in their thoughts, that if they could choose, they would **never** leave me, but the natural way of creation was for the children and the parents to release themselves from one another in the way, and in the time, that is in sync with each species. Nature's way, they told me, believes it would only weaken me if they did not let me go. They told me that they sensed this change, this *something*, was coming very soon, and it hurt them knowing we would no longer be together. But they also instinctively knew that the feelings of sadness and the missing of one another would be gone, replaced by the driving force to enjoy life's freedom; mate; and produce more children! For me, they added, I too, soon would be spared the sorrow I felt today. They said they believed and even felt, a strong knowing that I would also be freed and then go on to live a wondrous, productive life! They hoped one day we would meet again. I tried to understand why this was supposed to be a natural and good thing for our kind. *'Why did a family have to be separated? Couldn't we change that since we were, after all, a new species? How could anyone or anything call it a good thing to pull a child's love for her parents, and a parent's love for a child, away? And how could that be considered best? Why couldn't we change that? Why couldn't we, who were smarter than the other creatures; we who could think things through and plan and control most our actions; why couldn't we change this seemly lower something, this evolution of species' nature of things; at least change it in our newly created species-self? We loved one another so much!* I couldn't quite grasp at the time, why their love for me could not over power this strange force they said would soon be coming inside them, pulling them away from me… and they then would not miss me…

The day did soon come, too soon; when they turned from me and flew away from the Island, leaving me all alone… I had been maturing in spite of my sadness, but still felt a great need to be near them; and as I matured, their parenting instincts diminished… We had lived in great sorrow, stress, and desperation, for all those six months of our separation between the dome. They had both spent years *before* I was conceived, living in a similar state of existence as I. Then mercilessly, when they had at last found something that brought them joy, it was taken away from them, throwing them into even greater sorrow! The only joy we ever had experienced was when we were together as a family. I still had the desire and feelings of need to be with them, but their ancient bird and reptilian DNA had took hold, canceling out their desire and need to be with me, and… to protect me. It, instead, led them away to once again, someday soon, start another family, **without me…** When that terrible day arrived, I watched them fly away, growing smaller and smaller in the far distance; everything in me crying out in unbearable emotional pain! Something in me was pressing hard on my heart and solar plexus! I could barely breathe. I felt sick and like I would die; and, I prayed I would… the hurt inside me, a sadness rotting in me, stayed for a *long* time. Why did I too not have that something come and spare me all this pain? Why did it not care about a child, and remove from me, as well, this desire and need; this terrible, over-whelming loneliness I felt for my parents? Why was *I* forgotten and abandoned from this numbing something; left instead to suffer the emotions and the memories in confinement alone? I cried out to my mother and father as they flew from me, *'Don't go! Don't leave me! Mother, Father, I am all alone! …I…am…afraid…'* But they flew on, looking back only once. They called back to me; my father shouting to me, *'Fear not our daughter! This is the natural way of things from our non-human ancestors! We will remember you!'* And my mother added, *'We must go. We do this Dear daughter out of love for you!'* How could this, that feels so wrong and cruel; that feels so hurtful, and sad; be out of love? It felt like the opposite of love…did they not love me anymore? What did I do to make them stop loving me and go from me, to perhaps never see or be with me again? I was very young; I was confused, and extremely sad; I was afraid; I was locked away… and…I was all alone…

The days went by uneventful, and the nights following made my loneliness worse. Food did not interested me anymore, and I spent most my time in my nest, relishing in the fading scents of my parents. When I was conscious I sat with my head drooped down, my eyes closed, trying to shut out the pain of the loss of my parents and their warmth and love. I'd imagine they were there with me, and that we played and laughed again at the silly humans and Scientists! I imagined my mother's strong and warm wings covering me, protecting and comforting me…but when I would open my eyes, they were not there; I was all alone… I *knew* they were no longer there, and that they never would be…Yet I tried to believe they were, for then perhaps they *would be*. Perhaps the Scientists would bring them back; or perhaps I would open my eyes and see it was but a bad dream and they had never left me…perhaps…

I began to believe I would *forever* be locked in that dome, and *forever alone…* I then wanted to cease to be.. I did not want to live even a tiny moment longer without love…without my parents. Oh how cruel to create without forethought of what could become and befall that which one creates! How cruel, selfish, and thoughtless, were those who had created us, and in doing so, created me, a child who could feel all the emotions, pleasant and hurtful, and *not i*nherit the numbing hormone of detachment that took away the instinctive desire and need to be with another! Not even the laughing Atlantian children with the tasty treats could cheer me up. They were able to throw treats up to me because my dome cage had been pulled over their city, after my parents had flown away; and because their city left a small front section of their clear dome open to toss morsels up to me. A guard was always at their dome panel ready to close it within seconds, should I try to attack or venture too close. I tried, at first, to allow the children and the treats to take my mind off of my loss and sorrow. I had flown in curiosity, several times over the city for a few days. I did enjoy the sights at the time, but only for a short while. I enjoyed the children for some reason; perhaps it was an instinct that told me they were young like me; and so I felt closer to them than to the adults. I was at first, cautious of the adults, but soon felt safe enough to fly closer. I even ate the morsels of meat and other foods they threw up to me. But after only two days, I lost interest in them and their food; the sadness, too great to ignore... It was after the second day of flying over the city, and the Scientists seeing that I perched on top of their largest building, that of one of the royal family's buildings, and did not move from there for days, that they decided to return the dome back to my nest where it had been. There I rested my neck on the side of my nest, observing them for a while and their doings. The Scientists must have been concerned that they would lose me to starvation for they began to try and entice me to eat. I would not. I began to grow thin and weak; and the comfort of the unconsciousness of sleep called me to her inviting 'bosom'. Nothing, not even sleep, could pull me from the depression of my Soul and my entire being! Even in sleep, I dreamed as if I were awake; and so in my dreams I was still alone, *and*, I felt all the loneliness of it… There seemed to be no escape from my loneliness and misery…

It was several days after that, having not eaten in all that time, and while I held my head under my thick leathery wing trying to bury myself in deep forgetful unconsciousness, that I felt the Divine lite upon me, and begin to enter… *'Tü-Us-She'* I heard a soft whisper in my mind say. Suddenly I felt a change! I felt renewed and hopeful! I slowly opened my eyes, blinking them in curiosity. I took a deep breathe, wondering who spoke and what was happening to me! Suddenly I was aware of a presence; a loving presence, although I could not see anything around me, nor inside or outside my dome! I had lifted my head, looking around me and out towards the city. Just as sudden, I became aware or many things! I became aware, with understanding of the wrongs the Atlantians had done, and were still doing, and condoning! I also felt a strong emotion replacing the ones of depression, sadness, and loneliness. That emotion was compassion, deeper than before, for all those who had been, and those who still were being experimented on. At that moment I even felt pity and compassion for those who were *doing* the experimenting. I became aware of how they thought and felt and *why* they did the things they did, and *still* were doing! I now, somehow knew they had developed their own kind of prison; warren; and master; that drove them to do the things they did. I, for the first time, understood, with compassion and forgiveness, the Atlantians, and why they do what they do. It was *then* I was given my first color! I began to pulsate inside me the color red! That red glow pulsation inside of me lit up my insides as it lifted up my spirits! I no longer felt alone and sad. *At last* I was shown mercy! With this color I learned about life: consciousness of myself, life's passion to live, and its passion to become more! I too was life, and now I too felt the pleasures of life, but also the pain and separation *from* life and from the Divine! I learned the power of the passion to live and become more! The gift of red also stirred up the sorrows and the angers that were festering inside me, while they awoke in me joy! The gentle side of me began to have battle with the darker side of my emotions. They both seemed to fight to control me, to own me! *'But you are mine'* the true Creator, the Divine Eternal One/s, whispered in my mind! But due to the battle, and the conflicting emotional upheaval, I began the first step towards being totally consumed by these dark spirits of emotions: grief, anger, bitterness, hatred, depression, sorrow, loneliness, despair, and many others! I was plagued with both sides of these feelings! And then from these, rage was 'born'! Born from those dark entities of emotions and thoughts battling with the good thoughts! The emotions and thoughts of joy and pleasure were also consuming me! And both the light and the dark showed me that one entices the other; and so, I had to learn to utilize them both in ways that would complement creation, and bring about the best results. I went insane at times, with these conflicting battles; becoming a ragefull, mindless, killing machine! Sometimes ripping and tearing at the animal life inside the dome; feeling a frustrated need to bite and tear! My red gift was what some would call a blessing, and others would call a night-mare! I called them both...

For years, inside the dome, after receiving the color red, I had to learn the discipline of the emotions that the red invoked: the emotions associated with my thoughts, desires, frustrations, and the likes! It was during this time, after accustoming myself to the powers of the red light and the learning of its gifts, that I experienced its greater temptations, and its attempts at power over the will, my will... I failed the testing, allowing it to consume me with fiery passions, desires, and lusts! I had given in to the lust and the savagery of it all.

I was given many opportunities to learn the good of the order of things and its flow, and the discomfort of chaos that accomplishes the lack of discipline of both; *all* that was derived from the red-ray! I failed many of the challenges, allowing my emotions and thoughts to consume me with their fiery passion of desires and lusts! This was all new to me, so it over-powered me! I gave into lust, attempting fornication with other species, even though they were far smaller than I! I gave into the savagery of it and its passions and strong need for possession that went with it! It was *then* I had my first 'death' and burned up in my ego! It was my first death of my body, and that which I held in conscious. I had consumed my own self in the passions of desire, and thus, fell into self-consumption of ego! I began to glow redder and redder, until a flame began within me and out of control! Soon after that I went up in flames of a fire that combusted from within me, burning and expanding outward, burning, and consuming me rapidly to ashes! The fire was so hot that it took only mere seconds to reduce me to gray-black ashes! The pain was beyond my relating, and so intense that I was out of my mind with agony; sending me out of my body for release! I was one year and three months old, Earth time. That would be equivalent to fifteen years of age, in human terms. That is how I got my release from my prison inside the dome, and gained my freedom...

When I had turned to ashes, they no longer needed the dome barrier that had held me and my parents all those torturous years that we had been held prisoners. The dome was then removed, and my ashes reached for the heavens, carried on the ocean breeze, flying free to go, not where I might have taken myself, but where the *wind* took me... *yet*... they, I, were free! *I* was free! Free, at long last!

The Atlantian Scientists and Geneticists as usual, before this, had been observing me and my changes, fascinated; and so they had witnessed my burning! They must have been greatly surprised at my burning up, for they examined the area in which I burned, but found nothing that could have caused it; only my ashes. This normally would have been the end of me in this world. *I* thought so; the Scientists and Geneticists thought so; and anyone else who would have witnessed my burning, would have thought and believed so! But, it was not…instead the Spirit within me, now released, met with the Divine! The Eternal Divine Shinning One/s spoke to me in the most gentle and loving of voices, *'You have just experienced the powerful force of life when it begins its search for life, searching for its self. It has experienced duality of your world; turned full circle, and "bitten its own tail"! In searching for its self, your tangible self's place in life, and what and who it is, it but found itself lacking, consumed by its own selfish greed and desire for more of itself; for more of the power of its own selfish power! It consumed itself rather than sharing with the other aspects of itself: all life forms of different colors and gifts! You have now learned the first lesson in becoming what you **truly** are, and still are to become! You and **all** life are meant to become **all you can be** with what you have learned, earned, and have become at each point of your creation, and then again return to me! Each time you and my other life forms advance and ascend, all earn more of what they are to become! You (all) keep advancing!*

'You will now rise from your ashes of yesterday and be reborn to be given another chance to master the power of the red energy spectrum so to advance to the next ray: the orange ray, which is birthed from the red ray when it finds the light from the Golden Soul to tame and blend with it. You will therefore, be given another body like the one you had previously so to better learn the discipline that will in time, be a blessing to you and to all life and all mankind! And you will have stored within you all that you have experienced, and what you have gained from those experiences: pleasant and unpleasant. You will retain within you all the knowledge and wisdom of right and wrong choices, forgotten, yet there; until when you truly

*are readying and willing to retrieve them for the betterment of self and for all life! You, I now call Tii-Us-She! You were formed and altered by the Nephilim-Annunaki-Atlantians, who used my creations without my permission! So, you are Tii-Us from the city's name: Alan-ti-us! And, you are female! You therefore are She, the beginning makings of the Rainbow Phoenix I and you are giving birth to! When you 'burned' you were at 'Dead's Door', almost exiting from not only the dome that imprisoned you, but from the Earth's plane! But life continues on. And for you, life will also continue on, many times, again on Earth! This red Earth ray spectrum was the first color you were to learn before your first re-birth into the special life that you are being given. I have taken back all my creations that were put into you by the fallen ones; and I have now named you! Therefore, you are mine! And for a special purpose throughout all eternity! I shall forever protect you, enhance you, and deliver you safely, through the 'fires' of purification, to perfect you and bless you! You will accelerate at a high speed, enabling you to be my advocate and disciple of purity, so to assist the many worlds I have created. This will be done through the process of receiving and accessing the light enhancement, and the Divine Memories of the Sacred Truths I have encoded in you and in all that else I have created, and all that I **continue** to perpetually create! Tii-Us-She, your journey has just begun!'* With those words the Divine Eternal One/s put me to 'sleep'; and next, immediately it seemed, I awoke, not in the shell of an egg, but mature and full grown…*and, free,* outside of Atlantis! I then flew and found a place to rest for a time while I contemplated all that was told to me, and all that had happened in my experiences, so far.

Those who had created me, and those who remembered me from that time, did not know it was I, the same flying creature the Geneticists and Scientists had created over twenty-five Earth years ago and had kept confined in, and under, a great dome; for I had changed in features, color, size, and vibrational frequency! I had grown over those years to forty feet in height and ninety feet across in wing span!

My color was now, in my second life, ashen-black like the ashes my body had burnt to... that is, until I would become passionate in one form or the other; and then I would pulsate, or glow softly, or brilliantly, the color scarlet-red! My being now vibrated at a higher frequency than my last life time, extending my aura four hundred feet out and all around me! The people of Atlantis had been frightened of me at first, and I believe the Scientists and Geneticists thought I was an off-spring of my parents; and indeed I was! Only they did not realize I was the *same* one that inside their in-cage-ment had burnt to ashes! Well, same, yet *not* the same... I believe they noticed the similarities of my parents, and the old me they had experimented on; yet they had to have had also noticed the differences as well! It was not just my size, nor the color I was, but the other features I now had, that caused them not to recognize me. My features had changed because I was no longer the creature they had once created! I was now the Phoenix! I was different from my parents, even *before* the Divine Eternal One had 'touched me' and enhanced me with Divinity! The Atlantian Scientists and Geneticists had done additional alterations on me that they had not done on my parents. Remember, they had mixed within me, the DNA of the ant; the large sword fish; the bat; and 'the food of the gods': the algae! I had, besides that, the DNA Of the lizard, and the large beaked bird, which they had also taken DNA from, creating my parents; and they had mixed the DNA of the 'gods', taken from those pure-blooded Nephilim who ruled the city, combining it with the DNA of all the other life forms used to create my parents and I! They had also embedded within us crystal stones from the mineral world that had lain within the Earth and sea! I therefore, not only had the gene-pool which had produced my parents, but I also had the gene-pool family of **all** that lived within and upon the Earth: those that swam; flew; crawled; slivered; and had dominion… *and*, I had the alien's DNA; that being the Nephilim-Annunaki-Reptilian-Atlantian gods' DNA!

Soon the Atlantians loss their fear of me and began to look actually forward to seeing me. I must have been a great sight to behold in the sky for many besides the children. Many of the people would point and smile, making delighted gestures and sounds when I flew near and across! That's when they first began to toss food to me in my new form. They would toss up to me, on occasion, fish; small morsels of meat; bread; and some fruit and vegetables. The children especially loved to watch me catch what they threw up to me! Soon, I began to be like a mascot to them; a protector; and indeed I protected that city and its' people in spite of what the Scientists, Geneticists, and those in rule did and allowed to be done to me, my parents, and other innocent beings! But after a time, the angry side of the red color influence began to pulse and grow redder and brighter inside me; pulling me down and into it; activating the passion of old angers towards the Scientists, Geneticists, and Rulers of that city! That anger began to fester, and soon grew into hatred with the desire to rip and tear and destroy! I wanted to rip and tear apart those who had done my parents, I, and all the others great wrongs and harm! I wanted to destroy all they had used, and could still use to inflict their harm and mastery on! It was all I could think about! The other side of my Soul, the side of peace and goodness, tried to resist, and so both sides battled, creating a rage of insanity which threaten to consume me! I knew then if I did not control those emotions I would burn again! So I incredibly, mustered up enough strength to depart from that city, its people, and all areas close to it! But awww, the children... their gentle hearts, and innocent Souls, with their joyful, caring laughter... I miss them!

I found food, shelter and drink. I tried to spend my years alone, and away from others. I believed I could trust no one! I spent twenty seven Earth years isolating myself from others, and alone with my thoughts. My thoughts kept turning to all my pain and unhappy experiences. My mind seemed to play those reels over and over again, even though I thought I was not thinking upon those times and thoughts. It was not long after that before I began to glow red again with the overpowering control of the angry red influence. It was then I flew from the Atlantian city! It was about ten years after that departure when I had begun losing the battle of controlling my thoughts and the rage that came with it! I became consumed with my dark thoughts, which polluted my emotions! The negative thoughts and emotions were constant, never leaving me…and so, I went up in flames! This time flames of red and orange! The Eternal Shinning one now again spoke to me, *'I shall deliver you to peace, beyond time, where you shall live your life for a moment and a thousand of thousands of years all at once! There you will exist learning to master the seven lower rays of the seven lower worlds; thus, gain more understanding and knowledge of your precious lives, and all that has transpired before you and to you! These experiences, earning you understanding and knowledge, shall then deliver you into the "hands" of wisdom! When I return you back again to Earth it could be thousands of years in the so called pass, present, or future; or it can be in less than a click of a minute second; no time loss! All three exist at the same time, in the same space of existence, where I shall take you, as they do everywhere, but unseen, and unaware, in and to the world of matter! I shall return you to Earth, but not back to the present time there, nor its pass, nor to Earth's far future of a thousand plus years; but again and again shall I send you forward a few years, or a hundred years at a time, for tens of thousands of years, to Earth; and then to other worlds; until you have mastered* **all of** *Earth's rays, their weaknesses, and their strengths, gaining* **true** *wisdom!'* Then the Supreme Total All paused for me to grasp the understanding of the words. S/He began again, *'Now, my beloved Spirit, tell me what you have learned from your Earthly experiences!'* I then thought long, and searched in my memories for what I had learned that was of an importance. *'Let me help'*, the Eternal Shinning One/s said. My memory bank was then opened and the images of all I ever did, thought, or said, plus all I had seen, heard, felt, smelled, and tasted while on Earth, came pouring forth like a movie before me! Not only did I experience my own sense perceptions and deeds, but I also experienced and felt **all things,** and what those I had come in contact with had felt! I felt the joy of it and…I felt the hell of it! And, in agony, I trembled! *'Sleep young Spirit. Fear not! To rest I deliver you: to The Chambers of No-Thoughts, then soon after, The Place of Soul Enhancement!'* I then was put to 'sleep', and when I awoke again, I was well rested, refreshed, and calmed! I had awakened from that resting place of No-Thoughts, and was now in the bright, shinning plane of Soul Enhancement…

I peacefully existed in joy, peace, and love, in that plane the Eternal One/s had delivered me to, learning many things, experiencing many things, for hundreds of years there; yet merely only a year or more, if experiencing Earth's space and time continuum! I finally had mastered the lower seven rays, and so they were now mine, so to speak. They became an embedded/encoded memory, therefore, a natural, instinctive part of me! Hundreds of years I spent in that special place of light and dark; it made me strong in many areas of existence. I knew of the universe and its purpose, and I gained a love so powerful that it instilled me with wisdom of the dark as well as the light; coupled in a trinity of knowledge, understanding and unconditional love! It gifted me empathy; sympathy; and compassion, among so much more; more than I could relate to you here on Earth, for it was *beyond* the Earth human-mind's existing frequency, and its capability of vibration, so to activate the brain into comprehension! This was due to the frequencies in which you and your world exist at the present time. There, in that world of Spirit, where the Supreme Eternal Shinning One/s: He and She: androgynous: The Supreme Being, had delivered me, was a place where I vibrated, lived, and experienced life at a higher light frequency capable of understanding and remembering **all Those many things**! All that now, here on this plane of existence, I cannot! There, in that heavenly place, **all things were known at once**! Everything was like a paradox, occurring at once, yet separate! Things moved slow, yet rapidly; shone brightly, yet darkly! There, Opposites: the counter-parts/dualities, that existed on Earth, blended, becoming one, yet individualized! There were no separations there! Everything was normal and made sense to me; yet here I cannot grasp it! It does not make sense to me now, nor seem possible…and the memory of all I had learned there, had retreated into a deeper and unused section of my brain, not lost, but being stored there! I was told by the Eternal One/s, that those experiences, knowledge, and the wisdom gained from being with them were deposited/encoded into my DNA and Soul blueprint to be released, (bit by bit, when needed, and when I am ready and had gained a higher frequency of light;) into my conscious awareness. I was told, what was needed, or wanted by them and my own Soul needs, would then be given back to me, into my conscious awareness, at the right lifetime and moment when I have accomplished the things that earn me the ability to contain on Earth, some of that Sacred knowledge, understanding and wisdom! I also was told, and obviously been given, the memory to keep conscious, that I, as **all beings** on Earth and the many worlds, the Eternal One/s have created, would all have to go through the eternal 'fire' of purification, being cleansed; burning off all the toxins of the negative influenced thought forms, emotions, and deeds, accumulated; removing what needs being removed from our pure intend of Soul. The Sacred Purification Fire is not like the tangible fires on Earth that tangibly burns only the flesh, renewing not that which it consumes; but a symbolic fire, that cleanses the Spirit, preparing it for its return to its Soul and true itself, the Supreme first light, and then back to a worldly flesh renewed, to practice and experience life's desire to co-create, and then unify as one with all life, moving back again and again to and within the One, the Supreme, One True first light and creator of life! Again…something to contemplate much on! And indeed I did…

The Supreme returned me to Earth with this parting message, *'You have been here for what you, when on Earth, would have experienced as hundreds of years. Yet here there is no time; for here, in this Spirit world,*

we have allowed you to yes, experience a bit of time that has made it seem to you as but a single year away from Earth! I will now send you back and it will be, on Earth, but a single year you will have been gone! Know that all that I do has its Divine purpose; and you are being created, time after time, and beyond time, on the Golden Path that leads you to that purpose.'
With that I again awoke to a matured me, but **now** I was Green of body, and glowed with a lighter shade of red.

It was during this time of the second red burning, and my second re-birth, that I decided to venture far away from the city. I had now spent in my last life time, twenty Earth years over and around that city; and after my re-birth, five more years! You may wonder if I ever saw my parents again. Yes, I did, but not until I was full grown. It was a little over thirty years, in Earth's time continuum, before we met again. I had then existed, for over two thousand years, in true reality: the higher plane; yet here on Earth's plane of existence, it was calculated as only a little over thirty years…and, I was in the red, full swing! In this spectrum of the red-ray I was learning of the red fire of passion for, and of life, and conscious awakening: being more aware of myself! This entailed not only my experiencing the power of the influence these passions, hormones and pheromones had over me and others, but also it included the training and the developing of an awareness of them, and their power of over-taking a body! This was not only necessary in order to learn to discipline the raw emotions of the primal sexual drive/hormones/pheromones that drive all creatures to kill, and, or die for, under the untamed red's command and control; but also to learn of the passions of anger; rage; hatred; jealousies; insanity; and the other negative and destructive emotions and thoughts; but also including the positive ones, which are also influenced by the red as well! I will not take you through all I went through to learn to master these rays I was to experience and learn from, for it would take thousands of your Earth years to tell! But master the rays I eventually did! It took many hundreds of years of your Earth time, there on Earth, but I had the long life DNA encoded in me, so I was still young by those standards, with much time to learn; plus I had been gifted with eternal life! I would never die; never cease; until the Eternal Divine chose to change my Phoenix essence into another light; into another form of essence; therefore, *still* I would live on for *all* eternity...

I had to also go through the red-orange spectrum and know its gifts of light well...becoming it! The red-orange ray balanced my lust and my passions, causing me to want to create life to share with! I glowed internal the color of red-orange, and my body was the color blue-green! In this orange-red influence, I began to experience desire! That emotion of desire had begun to turn into mindless, uncontrollable, sexual desire! Again I gave into selfishness, caring for only my own needs and desire to please **me**! *I was* thoughtless of others and *their* needs; thoughtless of how my own selfishness, and desires, could affect others in a negative, hurtful, and/or, dangerous way! It was during the influence of the red-orange rays that I came upon my parents...

As I had said, I pushed myself hard away from my anger, hatred, and bitterness, so to be able to leave that great city of Atlantis! I did not want to consume them, nor myself, with the results of these raw emotions and thoughts! Succeeding in this, I then flew away from that city; flying every day; resting little, so to be rid of that city and its negativity that triggered such painful and violent emotions and sorrowful memories in me! I had evolved to where I needed very little in the ways of rest, sleep, food, and drink. I had evolved to this through my will, and because of the Divine's will; and from that, learned! The experiences in the far away, high frequency, dimension, that they, the Divines, had sent me to, for the learning of the control of the seven Earthen rays, and their powerful, and the abilities I was earning. I could then fly for days without the need for those things of substance! I would, however, stop out of habit, and desire, to slow down the scenery to look and experience what was around me, and what I had never experienced before now. I observed many life forms, and could identify similarities and slight differences in them. All this provoked inquiring thoughts and questions! I spend time with those thoughts, and would sometimes even walk on the ground getting closer looks at not only different animals, but also of plants, rocks, and those life forms that crawled, and those that slivered in a forward spiraling motion across the Earth. This too gave me thought, and I would spend hours questioning, contemplating, and pondering upon these things! From doing this, I gained better knowledge and understanding of the Earth, and the life upon her; all sharing the same world of existence! It took me months of travel, before I came upon a species similar to me. I had been flying, trying to control and discipline the red and the red-orange rays that often tried to send me mindlessly into their depths! These rays had been tempting me with the membrane of the feelings of the elation of dark release, along with its calm satisfaction after wards, which I had experienced in the pass, and at the times when I could *not* out-master it! At those times I had given in to the anger living in my memory created from the wrongs I held locked in my thoughts. I had not *yet* been able to pull had stayed for thousands of years learning to mastered all the seven rays outside of and pull inside my whole being, so to completely and lovingly trust that *all* would be the way of right and peace for me; if I did **not** *allow* those feelings of the red and the red-orange ray to rule the outcome! I had to trigger the knowledge and the disciplined I'd learned in that other special world, and the abilities I'd gained from it, in order to have the memories released. I had to do this by way of disciplining my desire to give in to the thoughts and emotions of anger; hatred; bitterness; lust; selfishness; revenge; and all other fragments of the negative side of the rays of red, and those of the orange! I had to control with loving 'hands', the power of the rays; not allowing those rays, along with my emotions, to bring about needless and self-appointed drives of judgment, destruction and chaos! I was experiencing much in the ways of chaos and temptation! I was learning, among other things, the power of the red passion of anger; hate; rage; bitterness; and insanity; with its obsessive desire and need to possess; master; and control **everything**! But I was also learning the positive side of the red-ray and the orange ray of life, and its driving force for life to continue; along with its passion of the emotions, and its overwhelming hunger of the sexual drive!

I had been in flight, having traveled hundreds of miles away from Atlantis, when I came upon the first creatures so similar to me. As I came nearer to them in flight, they had turned, facing me. I noticed that they were very similar to my parents, more so than I. There were nine of them, a mixture of males and females. The females were larger than the males. Two of them, the larger ones, were one, female and one, male. They separated from the others and advanced slowly towards me, while the other seven settled in tree tops, and on the ground. I could sense these larger two were the alpha male and alpha female; mates; determent in a common purpose and goal; and, it involved *me!* I could feel also anger and distrust directed towards me. They were hostile! I could smell it, sense it, and even taste it! This triggered my defense mechanism, igniting my red fire to defend myself; mindless of the consequences! When they saw me change in color, I believe this increased their defensiveness, and sent the adrenaline pouring in them to ignite their flight or fight mechanisms… and, they were directing it towards the fight side of it! I could smell it strong and determined! I could feel it approaching insanity, with the protective, instinctive rage that was being mustered up to overcome whatever this strange creature before them, me, was, and to prevent any harm I might be about to deliver! I could taste and see love crossing that fine line to hate! I prepared myself; halting in flight, taking on a battle stance in the air! The male spoke first, his territorial instincts kicking in, *'Back away!'* For a split second something in me paused, for it remembered a voice from long ago... But it was, after all, only a second or so, not fully registering. I responded back, *'I have free will to travel the sky as I will, and when, and where I wish! Let me pass!'* *'Not* **this** *sky!'* the female shouted with anger! Again, something in me skipped, pausing for a mere 'split of a hair'; but this time, pausing again, a bit longer. Enough time for me to register it! But, before I could really think upon it, for even only one more second, they *both* advanced on me! As they advanced, the female was more of the aggressor; passing up her mate, and speaking now in a more aggressive tone! *'Go back and away from our home, or we shall aim to tear at your flesh until you yield or die!'* She had stopped within fifty feet of me. Her mate came quickly up from behind her, stopping next to her, both ready to do what she threatened! *'Try if you dare! But no one, nor no-thing, shall ever control, nor keep me from my freedom again!'* They then both shouted out at the same time: *'To the death then!* And all three of us, at the same time, charged towards one another to do battle to our death if necessary! They fought for their freedom of home, and safety for their family. I fought for the freedom of my home and life as well; but my home was to me the entire planet and myself! And... **my** biological family, was no more... I had nothing to lose, except my freedom to do, and go, wherever and whenever I liked! It was all, I believed I had to live for, and to fight for! We charged towards one another; our massive wings making thunderous sounds as they beat together in the wind in hurried, angered, flight! The seven younger flying creatures, male and female, stayed back, allowing the two alphas to do the fighting while they watch for any signal to join in! The three of us fought fearlessly and relentlessly! We inflicted wounds; many that bleed profusely, others temporary scaring! I pierced, and pulled, and ripped at their flesh, sending the tiny feathers that were on their heads and tips of wings flying! I aimed for the most vulnerable parts of their body; biting and tearing! Yet they hung strong! It was a fair battle, two against one, because I was much larger than them both. They bit me also, for they, as well as I, had two rows of tiny sharp teeth! They used their powerful beaks and jaws as well to inflict damage to my body and neck! They had a more difficult time doing that than I, for my skin was thicker than theirs, but their determination found some success! I had two punctures on the left side of my long neck and also on my right wing tip! They were smart, I realized, for it seemed they deliberately, with knowledge, and thinking strategy, sought out the thinner areas of my body to attack! I had success also, for, as I said, I was larger and stronger, and had thicker skin for protection, than they. The female remained the more aggressive, even though the male was ferocious and determined as well; so it was she I came in contact with first! I too went for the throat, and she went for mine at the same time! We were locked in each other's grip, shaking our heads in attempt to rip the flesh and bring about either a death or wounded retrieval! She released me for I was going deeper into her thinner neck, but she did not completely withdraw! Her mate had come up around and behind me, planning on taking me off guard; blocking my retrieval so he could inflict his signature of injuries, while also allowing his mate to inflict damage to me as well! He went for my more vulnerable back side, my bottom underneath the beginning of my long tail! That pain spun me around! My body's re-actions caused my long and powerful tail to hit the female, throwing her away from me, sending her, surprised, and tumbling, for a short distance! She quickly gained her equilibrium and charged at me, my back now to her! I had swung around to face the male who had wounded me, and inflicted the pain! He had then; reared up his talons, ready to pierce my eyes! But I had gotten to him first! I had turned, pulling my neck back! Then I forcefully extended my neck and head outward, aiming for his eyes! He was quick, and had pulled his neck and head low, off to the left, succeeding in dodging my attack for the eyes, and received instead, deep punctures to the side of his forehead! He then quickly moved out further away from me, to his left, and next to my right side! He tried to seize my right wing, but I had seen what he was attempting! So I pulled my wing towards my body before he could!

Meanwhile the female had a hold of my tail! It seemed I had to have a multitude of heads and eyes, as well as thick skin, large size, and intelligent know-hows in order to protect myself from their attacks! I actually, then, in the middle of battle, had the thought: *'Those Atlantian Geneticists, and Scientists, and their Rulers, will probably try and do that with the next creatures, or people they experiment on!'* I was, even in battle, that calm and confident, in spite of my anger, to be able to think upon other things! And I was that indifferent to my own life or my death; for I *knew* I could *never* die! Never would I die to what the humans, and probably these two I battled, thought was a permanent forever after, ceasing to be; so I had no fear, and that fueled me on! I, still in battle, wore the 'red-hat' of the word: hatred!

At one point it seemed they were getting the best of me! But I had a strong, long-time anger, and bitterness, in me that the red, out of control, fed increasingly in me! I had those emotions from the memory of the loss of my parents, freedom, and the family life I had enjoyed for such a short time! I also held those negative emotions for the Nephilim/Annunaki-Atlantian Geneticists, Scientists, and Rulers who had caused so much grieve, and had done so much wrong to me and my family, and to the other innocents! Those hateful and bitter emotions had laid quietly inside me for a time before I came across these similar flying creatures. But now as the battle continued, my emotions were approaching being out of control and ghastly alive, attacking whatever was in my way! I fed on it, fueling myself in strength, stimuli, and the determination for success! I could tell that the two I did battle with, were surprised, for they were experiencing my great strength and anger, along with seeing and feeling the brighter and darker shade of the red light that was visibly glowing, and beginning to expand outward! They had, at first, jumped back in surprise, and a bit shocked! I knew they had never seen, nor experienced, something like me! And indeed, they could not have! For I was the first! They soon however, recovered, advancing; but a bit cautiously, on me again! They separated, the female again zooming in for my tail, while the male went for my face! I whipped around hard and fast to my right! Hitting them both, and sending them both tumbling in the air! They quickly gained their composure, and flew back to do battle; fighting desperately for their territory and their family's safety! The male tried to distract me from the female, while she circled me; also trying to distract me from the male! I first began to circle towards the female, and then, quickly, back to the male! But then, I remembered... I had to focus and stay calm! So I stopped, and hovered in one spot, allowing my excellent puerperal vision to observe them both, while I remained stationary; calmed, focused, and stilled! Just as the male tried to strike from my left side, I quickly whipped my tail around and at the female! While at the same time, I lunged with my pointy, colorful, beak opened, at the male; catching him unprepared to defend his self! I found my target, and had ripped a mouth full of flesh from his chest! It was slowly spilling his life blood! I had managed to hit the female, with my tail, at the same time! I heard the breath go out of her in a loud puff, as she again went tumbling backwards over herself, and away from me! She was now even angrier than before! I could smell and feel it increasing as she steadied herself with a look that spoke of her hatred towards me and angered determination to win this battle and send me away *forever* from their territory! As she again began to quickly fly towards me, her mate had already advanced just moments before her! He and I were already neck to neck in battle, attempting to inflict great and deadly harm to one another! We spun around several times; claw-locked, in mid-air; holding fast onto each other's foot claws, while our beaks, and front claws, pierced flesh; ripping and tearing at each other's necks, shoulders, chests, and whatever our beaks could grasp hold of! Neither one of us wanted to be the first to release. Even if one did, the other would probably go down too, holding on, caught up in the frenzy of the adrenaline! I not only had all this to contend with, but also the female who was full of rage by now and focused upon me and the goal of my death! She hit me with full force, from behind, hard, with the force of her full body weight, and the strength of her rage! It caused her mate, and me, both to be knocked forward, yet not apart! As she made to charge me again, only this time, with her talons, I waited, aware of her and her intentions, while I continued to battle with her mate! Just as she readied to pierce me through with her sharp talons, I spun around, still holding on to the male... And, she got her mate instead! He reflexively released me then, being only mindful of the sudden sharp pain, and the shock her talons had delivered to him! The weight of his downward fall caused my claws to loosen their grip on his! That's when the female turned from me, and towards her mate. She quickly flew down and beneath him, spreading her strong, thick wings wide! She was a good ten or more feet larger than him, so she was able to cradle him on top of her back, supporting him with her wings. She flew him to a nearby large and massive tree top where he was able to reach out to the thick tree limb, with his beak, then his claws; removing himself from her back, and onto the tree. I heard him say to her in gasps of breath, *'Just a few moments, to gain my strength and I'll begin again...'* The look they shared was one of such tender love and concern that it stayed some of my fury, so touched by it was I. And a seeping memory, I could not yet recall, yet it tried to seep in; also caused me to pause... I almost felt pity and tenderness for them both! But then the female turned her head towards me. She eyed me with yellow-red slanted eyes of hatred; piercing eyes; threatening, and warning me, that I had *now* crossed some invisible boundary line with her! I understood, for I had caused her to harm her mate, and that meant she would not yield to killing me, even if it meant the death of her! She was deep now into her maternal instincts, protecting those she loved! She eyed me fiercely while guarding her mate protectively; her neck extended with determination; studying me; working a strategy of attack! For a few quick moments I envied them, and a longing began to stir within me. It reached down deep inside me to pull up some pleasant memory... I then began to feel a forgiving nature surfacing, with a strong desire to be a part of their family. I observed them, not advancing. The male began to slowly raise himself up, testing his strength. He then slowly stretched his wings out, testing them also. The male then dared a test in the air, while his faithful caring, mate guarded him; a look of concern now on her face. And I stood my ground, not advancing, while I quietly observed all this. It intrigued me, and if they noticed or sense my emotional change, they did not acknowledge it. Instead, they kept their determination, and the female kept her aura of hatred towards me! It was so strong and hostile that it would have sent an enemy fleeing, if that enemy had not been me! I could see and sense the male's pain, but he too was determined to rid his family of this intruder! Me! Even through my own anger, I remember thinking, *'How brave and protective they are! This kind of love I have never seen, except with my own parents and me'.* They had begun to remind me of my parents from another life time, long ago. Again, with those thoughts, I felt a tinge of longing to be with my parents, and be loved as much as these two before me, loved one another and their family! I could tell that the female was much in concerned for her mate and his injuries, but she was trying to cover it up with the emotions of anger and hate! She then shouted to me, *'Yield!' 'Never!'* I shouted back! I then shouted, *'I have earned my freedom, and my right for my hatred towards all who would try and inflict limitation and similar treatment done to me and my loving parents! My anger is strong against those I fly from who live in that great city of mutilation and selfish cruelty! I'd sooner cease to be than allow another to control me! Inflict all the injuries and pain you* **think** *will stop me! But it will not! For I have experience worse! Let the battle commerce, if that is your desire and goal for me!'* I then thrust my neck forward, pulling my back legs close to my body, extending my talons, preparing to charge them again! But the female and her mate stayed where they were, and looked at one another with a look of surprise and questioning; their energy changing. The Female shouted out: *'Stop! 'Stop I shall not!'* I shouted in reply. *'Stop I say!'* the female had again shouted! And the male shouted right after her, **'Please** *stop!'* I saw and felt their emotional frequencies change again, as well as their expressions! When the male had said **please stop**, I thought it meant they yielded. The female's expression of hatred had changed so swiftly that it puzzled me, and I wondered if it were a trick. She began to very slowly fly towards me. I could feel she was contemplating on me and something else. I prepared myself for any trickery she may have planned; watching her every action while using my far away vision to watch the male. Was this a new tactic to destroy me? *'Why do you say stop, and yet you approach me?'* I asked the female suspiciously. *'What trickery is this?'* She only looked at me, studying me, as if she were looking deep within me. 'Daughter..?' she asked. *'Daughter?'* I questioned myself. *'What is this?'* I asked her; and then in the next moment, miraculous recognition came to me! *'Mother?'* I'd questioned out loud! *'Perhaps,'* she said slowly, but with the smell of excitement! Then she studied me a bit longer, and I could feel and smell the excitement in her, rising! *'Were you birthed inside a large clear dome outside a great shinny city in the sea?'* the male asked me. I was now excited as well, my heart racing! *'Yes'* I answered. *'And were you both'*, I asked, *'there, and then six months after you gave birth to a daughter, released from the dome, being separated from your infant daughter, now for approximately thirty years?'* I asked this, excited, and in anticipation of a positive answer! *'Yes!'* they both excitingly replied! And with that, the female rushed towards me laughing; this time rushing towards me not out of hatred, but out of love! The male slowly, in physical pain, followed her as quickly as he could, an aura of great joy replacing all their previous emotions and thoughts of animosity! They now embraced me, not to destroy me, but to hold me dear and close to their heart in love, not hate! I could feel their joy as if their parenting instincts for me had returned; and indeed they had! They told me that over the years, their crystal implants had aided them in developing the higher qualities of their Soul to such a level that their desire to be with me again, as a family, had returned to them, and now they could control, to a larger degree, the power of the pulling away from their off-springs! They also told me there was a 'price to pay' for those qualities they had gained. They said that 'price' was the gift of memories and the emotions that went with it. They said they had all the memories of our time together; and through the gaining of memory, and the higher qualities of the Soul, they *again* would feel, every time they remembered, the emotions of strong love for me, and also the pain of not being able to get to me in the dome. **And** they would remember and feel the strong painful desire to set me free, along with the sad frustration that they could no,t and may never see me again! They told me they even felt time and time again, **all** the memories of the great sadness and grief, they had gone through when they could not find me to set me free and be with me again! Plus, they felt **all** that was attached to **all** the pass memories they held inside. *'We had left care of our family, and the alpha position, with the wisest, strongest, and bravest members, while we flew back to that city. We had embarked upon that plan and journey soon after those memories and desires were given birth again. Our plan was to set you free and to bring you back here to be with us and your family. We were in loving joy and great hope of seeing you again; and succeeding in our plan to have you back! But when we arrived there, after over a month of travel, the dome was no longer there, nor were you... We feared you had perished. It was eleven months, after we departed from you that we arrived at that city again in hopes of finding you. You would have been seventeen years old at that time that we had gone back for you. Some of our grief was subsided, but never did it stop, by telling ourselves that perhaps they had decided to set you free, as they had done us; or perhaps, you escaped instead, and we then had a* **real** *chance of meeting you again!'*

We flew to the ground, the others following with looks of confusion on their faces, whispering and mumbling to one another! Once we got to the ground, in a clearing, my parents began again questioned me, *'You do not look much like the Dear daughter we had to leave behind; but I sense you truly are. And what you have just verified for us, tells us you are she; but why do you look different from us; and why do you glow and have color?'* I tried the best I could to explain these things to them and the family members who were listening to us. Then *I* asked questions. *'Are all these others then, my brothers and sisters?' 'Yes! She said happily. Come, Dear Daughter, meet them!'* My parents then lead me over closer to them, and introduced me as their sister, and my parent's first born! They told them I was the long lost daughter they had been seeking all these years...

My parents wanted to know what all had happened with me since they had last seen me. My brothers and sisters were happy to meet me, and were also full of questions for me! They all began to question me at the same time! My parents said, in a voice of happiness, *'Everyone be quiet for a few moments! Let her rest...and us, for we have battled, and that, and the wounds, have weakened us. We need to have water, lie quietly for a few moments, and fill our stomachs. Let us take care of these things first. Save all your questions for then. We can gather, after we dine, and then share all we want. Come; come children...'* She said this, including me, with so much happiness in her Spirit, and voice, it could be strongly felt by *all* of us! I was now happy... She turned to me as we walked, following her instructions. *'Come my Daughter...'* and she stretched out her right wing towards me. At that moment, I had a flash memory of a warm and protective wing, and so found myself instinctively moving to snuggle underneath her extended wing. I, almost shyly, instead, stepped not under her wing, but forward towards her side; towards my father; and then towards my new family... I was home! I was, at *long last,* reunited with my loving parents! My few pass moments of wishes, during battle with them: that this *was* my family, had come true! I had found my birth parents, at long last! I was ecstatic with joy; my two hearts feeling as if they swelled, in the most beautiful and pleasant way, ever possible; filling up with love for *all* things! All bitter, and hateful emotions, and thoughts, fleeing! I felt *truly free* for the very first time! We embraced, so filled with joy! Our necks entwined together, rubbing each's neck gently. Our wings spread to allow us closer contact! My anger and hatred at last, subdued; my rapid pulsating, red glow, appeased, subsiding to a soft gentle pulsation of pink! *Oh, how my Soul and two hearts sang: 'I am home! I am* REALLY at long last *home'…*

My family of brothers and sisters must have been very surprised and confused when they had first seen us stop in the sky, in mid battle, and then rush together; not to harm one another again, but instead embrace and laugh; for they were too far away from us to hear our conversations. It was wonderful to have brothers and sisters, along with being again with my parents! For months all of us lived together in peace; happy there, together, free of the Atlantians, their doings, *and their evil!* I was truly happy with them, and that life time, for many years; soaking in all the beauty of love and feelings of be-longing… but then, after a time, I began to desire to mate! This was a new sensation for me! I had been going through the other facets of the influence of the red ray for close to two hundred years now, that is, if I counted the time in the higher bode of a heavenly place, and at this time of mating desire. That Earth life's time was also taking me into not only the red influence, but also the influence of the orange!

There were six females in our family, including my mother, and we were *all* in season to mate! Each females', including mine, mating cycle had synchronized with the most dominate female, that being my mother, the female alpha. Before very long, all of us females hit our cycle of desire's mastery, driving force, and availability to except a male and bring about off-springs. The males began to pick their females. Some wanted the same female. My father, being more spiritually and conscious aware, and advanced in many ways, like my mother, stuck with one another, choosing not one of their children to also mate with. We females also had our preference, and would give a warning sound, low in our stomachs and throats; puffing out our wings to those we did not choose. If necessary, we females would chase, and/or peck, even flocking with our wings, any male suitor we did not choose to mate with, who might ignore our warning! I desired, at first, only one male, even though he and the other males were biologically brothers. But I was experiencing the effects of the red-ray moving into the orange. I was beginning to glow red-orange, with the power and the drive to pro-create, and mother my own children! With it was carried the overpowering drive to mate and become one with any male that I chose! Still the 'red-fire' of lust was stronger in me than the orange, blocking out the mindfulness of the family blood relationship. Brothers began to fight for the right to have the female of choice to appease their maddening lust drive to copulate. The Pheromones coming from them, and myself, were strong, over-powering me and my control! When my sisters were rejected by every male, for they all choose me, except for my father, of course; my sisters, acting on the pheromones, began to desire to fight me! The males chose me because it was the natural order of choosing the strongest pheromones released and most aggressive and confident to have the male of choosing! And that I had! Whereas, the female would choose the strongest male for to produce strong off-springs, enabling better chances for their children to survive their birth and youth, and also to survive to maturity, and be able to produce their off-springs as well! The males knew I was also the strongest in other important ways, and that is one of the reasons why the females, my sisters, did not get a chance to mate. Even though they were my sisters, and I loved them dearly as my sisters, whom I would protect to my death, I was powerless to the drives that were taking over my system; and so I would have, at that time, fought them to the death.

I and my sisters soon began to fight! I no longer cared to seek out **only** the strongest male; I wanted them all! The females fought in a flock-pack, being sisters far longer than I, and having the exact same biological gene pool, but a lot different then I! They then worked for one another, and *against me!* There were four females, and so they thought they would be able to over-power and take me…they did not, and they could not… Even though this was my family in which I loved as a full blooded family blood tie related love, I still had blood that was different than theirs! For the Atlantian Geneticists had engineered other changes within me; including the combining of different species' DNA with the DNA of my parents! Therefore, the red-orange and the other different DNA over-powered, during this time, any sense of any family-blood ties and loyalties in me that I would have had, otherwise with the females. The red-orange tried to overtake me, and master me! ***It*** was now in control; and I was a fearless kill or die puppet!

'Children of Earth, I tell you all that I tell you, now, in the beginning, and throughout the entire *story, so you can understand and learn through my experiences and my story of how I felt; how others throughout the thousands of years felt and perceived things; and how others **still** feel and perceive things! All of this I have told you, and am continuing to tell you, is* important *to tell; important to and for you, and the entire human race! It is* important *for you to contemplate upon **all** in this story; and important to you to **remember…**'*

…I found myself battling to have ***all*** the males, rather than *they* battling for me! I became insanely greedy and full of myself! *'You are now the master of all of them!'* My emotions with the red-orange, and with the pheromones, seemed to say things of that nature to me! So I battled with my sisters, wounding them! I wounded two of them badly, almost killing them! After that, they backed away and gave me free range! I flirted and flew in circles around ***all*** my brothers, trying to entice them into fertilizing me! But then when they did come for me, I turned towards my own father instead! For he was the alpha, the strongest male in this flock-pack! My mother tried to discourage me or stop me by trying to calm and reason with me! She flew over to me as I was flying towards my father. They were both perched together high in a tree, observing my actions. I ignored her, shoving her away from me! I then began twisting my body; vibrating my tail and its small earned feathers at him! I threw myself at my father, coming close to his face with the back of my body; my tail held high up from it, trying to seduce him! He stood strong, not leaving the branch, not tempted! *'What is consuming you daughter?'* my father, much concerned, calmly asked of me. I did not want to speak, I only wanted action! But he now flew up, backing away from me, and spreading his wings across himself when I came close, blocking me from him! *'I* **have** *my life-time mate! Compose yourself! Take control!'* He said this in an alpha commanding tone to me! *'You* **can** *do this!'* Being that he was not only my biological father, but also the male alpha, my natural instincts woke me to my senses! But only for a short while! *'Father I cannot! That which has afflicted me has me held by my mating season's lust!'* *'You* **CAN** *take control! Remember who you are and all you have learned and have become!* **Will it!***'* Then he added with the alpha command, *'***Now!***'*

I tried to control it, I truly did! But it was difficult! So I began to glow more red, shifting from orange to red, than back to orange to orange-red, and then red again, in my attempts to control it! It, and the emotional shifts, was maddening! And I feared I would go mad or burn to ashes again! I wanted to control the drive, and yet **not** control the drive, so powerful was it! It, the pheromones, and the scent of mating, had me powerfully held in their clutches of lust, and the pull of the natural rhythms of natural reproducing! *'I will not fight you daughter!'* my father said will a stern but loving voice. *'But if you do not, or cannot master these drives, you must have the wisdom and strength to leave us and find a mate* outside *of this family! You are intelligent and wise enough to understand and know why.'* I knew it was what I *had* to do! I had to take with me these emotions with their natural lustful, driving way, of keeping the species continuing on, far away from my family, to protect them and protect their blood-line! I tried to calm myself, battling with the desires of the physical body, my thoughts, and the spiritual body, and, self. My wings flapped, my head moved back and forth, and up and down in my struggling attempts! I emitted strange guttural sounds that would erupt into loud shrieks! I even wept in my struggle with these drives! But leave I finally did. I flew desperately, without even saying good-bye! I flew quickly in my desperation to contain those emotion in a 'safe-box' inside me, and for their sake, separate myself from my family as fast as I could, in hopes they, and I, would at least gain some peace, if not I, a willing mate… I found not a mate, for there were none like me, and there were none like my parents and siblings. I flew for days before the urges subsided enough to allow me to desire to lite upon a mountain top. After traveling away from my family, still in the cycle of needing to mate, fighting the desire to return, and not finding any like species to mate with, I was 'forced' to face the powerful drive alone, or, to try and mate with another species…

In my travel away from my family, I encountered many different species of animal and reptiles. I eventually encountered two different species that flew and were closer to being more like me than any of the other species I'd ever seen! Today you, here on Earth, tell of them in your myths and legends. You call them: Thunderbirds and Dragons! The first *I encountered was a* female Thunderbird; and I later learned the other two I encountered were called Dragons! And they were brother and sister…twins!

We had seen one another, at first, from a far distance. The two Dragons were the first of the two large flying species I had encountered. The Dragons had first begun to circle me, coming slowly, closer; becoming more and more curious! They ventured closer each time! The male increasing his speed on his circling, as if excited! I was still in the mating mode, and he knew it, but seemed confused, as he would stop his approach, and observe me with questioning eyes. I knew I must have confused him greatly, for not only was I **not** his species, but I was a species unknown to any other living thing on Earth! I wanted to mate, and so did he! The female had stopped as well, not advancing towards me, but studying me. Her brother began to circle again, moving slower, yet closer to me, as if weighing his intentions and movements. We both began circling one another, he and I, attempting to communicate by way of our mind. We succeeded in communicating, and the male, let me know he wanted to mate with me! My season's call was calling him; drawing and igniting him, as it had my brothers! But then, that is another story... But one day soon, *they, and the Thunderbird, too* shall each tell you their story, and then, the four of us shall tell you the story of our meeting and adventures together! I will, however, tell you that the attempted mating was full of action in the sky! Fiery and thunderous! And, *not* possible... Finding no others like myself, I could not reproduce, so I eventually had to go off to myself and deal with these torturous and overpowering urges until they passed; alone, except for the Divine within me...

I could not fully contain all of the mindless drive to mate and reproduce, so I found myself *again* seeking males, and battling with other creatures weaker than I in order to try and get what I wanted; heedless and mindless of other's needs and the harm I inflicted in the process! And so it was that it was not long before I again burned! I burned up in selfish, thoughtless lust, that contained no consideration for others, nor how and whom I harmed in the process! I then had to learn again, on a higher plane, so I burned... I went up in flames! But interesting enough, not as hot as the last time! I burned in yellow-red flames, releasing tinges of gold earned from all the kindness I had previously learned and given to others. This Gold tinge blessed the burning and softened it! The flames then blended and moved into the color of orange alone, to then a bright orange! I saw images, my thought forms, 'swimming' all around, and above me in the flames as they were being released from my mind! I saw the life I had lived this time, and the lives I'd lived preciously before each burning, pass before me; and I heard and felt the agony of all those I had harmed, were indifferent to, or cruel to; and those I had killed, or had inflicted pain, or hardship upon! I saw through *their* eyes! I felt through their pains: emotional, mental and physical! I saw into the depths of their souls, and saw and felt *all* they had endured, all they had thought, felt, and experienced, both before, and when our paths had crossed! And I then knew *why* they did and said the things they did. I cried with their tears, and raged with their rage! I laughed when they laughed... and so died, when they died... It all came in excruciating waves, like contractions of birth and re-birth: all life's pains from thousands of years, bunched together, and worse than any physical pain I had ever experienced; and more real then what I had believed was real or possible! I had created, by my choices, by my thoughts, by my words, and my deeds; and, by my will, and my undisciplined nature, *my own* hell between lives! I now knew more about life and each life of everything; and so I learned more of good and evil, the Divine, and, myself... I was burning in the red-orange flames of my own hell from undisciplined emotions and drives of the worldly five senses! I was burning in the red and orange flames of my own created hell! But, I also had gained, for I *now* knew more about life and this dimensional plane, you here call: Earth! I now knew so much more of its pendulum swings from dark to light, and then from light to dark; discomfort and chaos, to joy and prosperity; then back again, to dance the dance of blending and mating! I had experienced the dark and the light, and along with it, what they and creation shares, and moves about, in their seeking of alchemizing life's mating of opposites into balanced perfection to better give life to life, and, *for* life! I experienced, so learned, of its *many* facets of expressions, mirroring beauty, in *all* it teaches and all it reflexes! Life turns you, things, and *all* creation existing on, and in, your world, around to all that it offers; to all it is; and all it can be! It turns you, and all it reflexes, up; down; all around; in; and inside out; *until* you grasp its understanding, gaining loving wisdom, and empathy, flowing *easily* with its 'waves, as you do its soothing currents... I was gaining knowledge and understanding of each life I had experience, and each life experience of those I had come in contact with, whether I had done harm to it, or them, or not. For in some supple way, I had influenced them, even just by my mere observation of them, for but only a second or less. And so, I learned of good and evil, and its influences upon those one comes in contact with; and how even the mere conscious awareness of another has its affects and consequences upon me, and all life! I learned more of not only myself, the Earth, and her life forms, but I also learned more and gained more, understanding of the Divine Eternal One/s…

I was then returned to another higher plane of existence; one higher than the one before; and I remained there for four years of Earth's time continuum, but equivalent to one hundred years in that other dimension of higher knowledge and existence. There, in that world, the Divine again spoke to me. *'You will be here in this place beyond time, for as long as it takes for you to adjust to your new experiences, understand them, and why you combusted again. You will also stay here until you can forgive and emphasize with all the life and its many forms that you had interactions with, and experienced, in your last life time before you were returned here. You must give away your animosities towards life, others, yourself, and circumstances; emptying out and replacing those void places with self-love, agape love, and the will of intent to do no hateful or violent harm, nor be indifferent to anyone or anything. Let your desire and intent be of compassion, and gratefulness, even when you consume substance, and when removing a life form to partake of its substance so that you and/or others may be able to eat to keep their bodies living on that plane of existence. When you have learned well all these things, you then shall be returned again to me and then to the Earth's other planes to* learn also from there! This way what you experience while on Earth, will eventually raise the vibrational frequencies of your body of matter, which includes your mind and brain, which influences your emotions and spirit, higher with each time you return and learn the things of Earth you are meant to learn while there. You will continue going through all you have been going through until you **want to** raise, and have raised your frequencies high enough to be able to contain **all** the color rays! You will then continue to learn of the color spectrums of the light that governs and influences Earth, and all she gives birth to, and shares life with, there upon her! Until you do, and until you become them, and learn to control them, helping to balance life on the worlds in which I send you, you shall return again and again! There are much more that influences, **all** in each place of existence, besides the light spectrum! There are light influences from the individual stars, the planets, the many galaxies, and the gamma rays that are omitted forth from that which you see, and that which you do not see in the night sky or the sky of light! There is also the influence of gravity, magnetism, electrical influences, the elements, and air pressure! Plus far more influences, and affects, than you can know or understand at this time. By raising your body/matter's light frequencies, you will eventually have raised the body's frequencies high enough to allow it to be able to contain **all** the color rays, becoming them, and blending them with your aura and being; mastering them, thereby, helping to balance and raise all of Earth's light: an ascension of Spirit and Soul! Without the rising of the vibrations and impulses of the density of matter, you, nor any life there, or on any particular plane, cannot gain the knowing and innate desire to be closer to who and what each of you and I, **truly** are, and the existence all were created to experience and share with all life! When you are sent back to Earth, you will be leaving here having learned the beginning of the influences of the orange light ray. You shall go back to experience its magnetic drawing, along with the influences, and the spiritual and physical effects it has; not only on you, but other life as well! Plus, learn the *controlling of, and effects of gravity, polarities, and electro-magnetism has upon self and all life! You will learn of their causes and effects on you and other life, so to learn to discipline them, mastering self; protecting self; perfecting life; its influences; and your emotions! In the other color spectrums, you shall learn about thoughts, as well as the results that words, emotions, and actions have upon all of life! On the plane, known to many as, Earth, the Magnetic-Spirit will draw to you things, and beings, that you need to experience, so to learn more from. These are symbolic of a triangle's three points: all three points of creation! You will need to learn the causes and the effects of your choices. You are meant to learn what is needed to master, and to tame, in order to emerge and blend again into the 'heart beat' of* all *creation; and into the whole of the universes of all life that is, and perpetuates life! You will need to learn how to still the mind, controlling your thoughts, words, and actions...again, the three points of creation! As you now remember, you have, and will again, learn these things here on this spiritual plane, before going back to experience the effects of the three points that exist on the Earth plane. For all things are first learned and imagined here on the spiritual plane,* before *manifesting there, on Earth, or anywhere! When I send you back, you will have earned the gifts, and feathers, of the colors: red, red-orange, orange, orange-yellow and yellow. If you succeed to master, on Earth, all those rays, up to the green ray, by accessing your innate knowledge from your experiences here and on Earth; and you do not burn before then: being purified, in the yellow ray and yellow flame, before you reach the green ray, you will, when brought back here, have earned the right to receive the wisdom of the higher rays! The higher rays shall gift you knowledge, wisdom, understanding, plus the innate memory, and connection, to me, and the collective, which shall blend with the lower rays you have gone through on Earth's plane! This shall send forth Higher Spirit Guardians of those rays to assist and help you while you are on Earth. They will assist you in retaining, and recalling, much of what you have learned and earned there on Earth and here in the higher plane of learning!'* I then was put to sleep in the no-thoughts cradle, to awaken when I was well rested. I did not need to stay in the no-thoughts cradle-chamber as long as the last times I was there; for I had raised my consciousness high enough that the light I had earned rejuvenated me at a quicker pace! After again being in that holy place for another hundred years, which moved so rapidly that it was but only four years of Earth's time, I was again put to sleep. I awoke back on Earth, matured, fully grown, with extra wisdom and under-standing...but in another location other than the one I'd left when I had last burned to ashes! It had seemed not long, only mere seconds, after the Divine had spoken to me that I had awoken full grown and in a different location, far away from my parents and my family! I also was a different color of body, with a different glow internal. I went from a blue-green body to a blue body; and from a red-orange glow, to an orange glow! As I learned of the red-orange ray's properties, and passed their tests, I would glow yellow, and my body would change to Violet. In the internal glow of the yellow ray, and its counterpart: the glow of my violet ray body, I would switch from compassion, Divine Love, joy, motivation, intuition, and hope; to the counterpart emotions of hatred, resentment, depression, jealously, insecurity, sorrow, and similar emotions; only to switch back to their positive counter-parts again, and again; back and forth, making a full circle of ups and downs, until I was able to easily discipline them; combining them in such a way that they strengthened the continuality, and serene flow of mine, and life's essence! It was the ray that glowed inside me, which held the most influence; and so it was important I learn to pull whatever color I needed, inside me! From the glowing yellow ray I was to learn of emotions and their power to control one in fear, or hate; or compassion and love. I had to learn all the influential emotions, both negative and positive! I learned how the emotions, when 'fired' with thoughts and beliefs, could instill positives, or fear and isolation, in many negative ways, from my Soul, other's Souls, and from the Soul of all Knowing! The gifts of beauty entail trust. This trust is trusting life, self, the Divine, and your Spirit and Soul that exists within you, that always exists everywhere, along with its singularity of unity which is always present, whether we are aware of it or not; and is **always** there helping and caring about ***all*** its Creation!

When, after many years of experiencing the yellow light's affects and powers, along with its violet opposite spectrum, and giving into them, rather than mastering them with my will; choosing to indulging in their delights of light and dark instead; I would then flame up and be sent back to the Holier plane, and then again back to Earth! Each time of my return, I would be a different body color, along with its counter internal glow; but in the same, or a similar body form! My internal glow would be of a next higher color spectrum then the last! My body would then be the counter-part color; balancing and nurturing one another.

It seemed not long, and before I had succeeded in learning much about the yellow ray of emotions, at its most powerful level, that I was tested. I was tested by my Soul, so that I would know how well, or not, I had learned; and if I now needed to burn up any polluted, toxic emotions that could be holding me back from reaching my higher potential. It was not me, of the flesh and blood that decided this, but the Divine Soul that dwells within me, and within the Creator of all things! For that Soul remembered *all* I had ever experienced and learned, but which the physical body and mind could not! It done to me, that which I, in this body of matter, would not of had the courage to do! So I was set to 'burn' again! Set to burn away that which was not needed and held me back from my Divinity! I was to shed all those toxins and begin again, purged by 'fire', given another chance! I had finally, that life time, learned of the influences and gifts of the lower rays' colors: red, orange, and yellow; plus their counter-colors. After that burn, and then the rest period in the higher abode, I had to return back to Earth to learn of the influence of the red glow and its green counter-color ray. With those colors I had to learn of the flesh and its needs and desires, along with learning to connect all of that with the Divine Spirit and the Earth herself! I had to connect to her, and all she was connected to! Once I had learned that when I would switch to turning orange of body, and internally glowing blue, I could then learn deeper truths about the Divine Spirit/Soul, Earth, and the power and influence of the word and manifesting, I then became more enthused and eager to learn more, and experience more; negative as well as positive! I also then was able to almost enjoy and look forward to the times I'd encounter struggles, for I knew it was a prologue to knowledge and blessings of all I could imagine and desire!

After spending fifty years of Earth time learning of the blue internal glow, and the orange of body, then burning, I awoke from the plane of Spirit and found myself resurrected back on Earth! But far from where I, with my family, had lived. I was resurrected in a land strange to me. My body was now orange-yellow again, and I would glow blue or green when excited, and red when upset! Four more years of Earth's time had passed, and I now found that I recalled my last life experiences, and... I recalled my parents! My parents had once seen me combust, and it had frightened them! I had tried to explain to them, over the months I had spent living with them, what had been happening to me, and could happen any time. I told them that the Divine granted me re-birth; and when the day came that I would burn and leave this world, being re-born back to Earth, I would try to find them again when I returned. I explained that I had to learn here on Earth, to control my emotions, thoughts, words, and actions, while learning from them. I had to go through this and do this because of a special Divine plan our Supreme Creator had for me, and for mankind. I had to learn control, and learn from **all** my experiences, before I would stop burning. I had the strong feel and longing for family again! I now remembered my promise to them: to seek them out when I returned! But it wasn't long into my search for them that the memories of them began to fade... I then no longer searched for them, for I had forgotten them… I was, after that, like a new born babe, searching and longing for something, but I knew not what. There was a great emptiness inside me. I felt loneliness again, and I felt need. By this time the orange glow, instinctively, had me missing and longing for family; togetherness; and love, without my knowing it was *this* I missed; longed for; and sought after; and which was creating the void inside me! Without being consciously aware of it, I also had these feelings of longing and emptiness due to my Spirit missing the blissful place where I had been; the place where I had felt and met with the Divine…

I had lived many more years after that, on Earth, experiencing the strong pull and influences of the orange color spectrum, along with its desires to have family, create family, and fulfill its need to search outside of me for something unseparated from itself. In my search I came across many different life forms; and again a species larger than I! It was the Thunderbird-She! We resembled one another enough to make me think we were cousins! And, indeed we were! We were double cousins! More like sisters than cousins. I will not tell you how that was possible, for that is *her* mission. It is her story for *her* to tell. Her mission of the telling of her story, to assist 'man-kind', as I am doing with *my* story and its reflections! This story I now tell is *my* mission to tell to and for 'mankind'.

The Thunderbird-She eyed me, but neither she nor I were in a sociable, or a threatening mood. So the first time we crossed paths, she calmly flew pass me, but let me know with her intense eyes, that she saw me. When, after many months, our paths crossed again, we studied one another from a distance, beginning to fly in our own private small circle so we could observe one another while not moving closer, but maintaining, while reserving, energy; yet also maintaining motion, in case we needed to move fast! She had the same face shape and neck as me; same kind of beak; same thick leather-like wings; same front and back feet and talons! I had three long colorful feathers on the crown of my head; she had two. My feathers were red, orange, and yellow; hers were red and black! I had no other feathers, except for small ones, same colors, on my wings and my triple tails. These were the colors I had succeeded in mastering in my many lives. I had earned by this life time, eighteen small pointy feathers on my three thin tails. They were the same three colors as the other feathers I bore. My middle tail was the longest. I had three feathers of red, orange, and yellow, on both sides of all three of the tails. She had a tail shaped like a opened fan, with multiples of black, red, and white, feathers; three or four times longer, and wider, than my tail feathers! Her wings were covered with feathers of various sizes, but the same color as her tail. My leathery bat like wings were covered with scales, shaped in curves, with sharp claws on the ends of each of their four sections. They had small feathers of red, orange, and yellow, sparingly on them, for I had to earn my feathers and their colors! The back ends of my wings curved towards the back of my body, and the front ends of my wings curved up towards my head. When completely expanded, each of my wings spread out approximately forty-five feet from my body, and curved about twenty feet in front of me, and twenty feet behind me; the claws pointing towards one another. This offered me protection should I be attacked from the front or the rear. The Thunderbird-She had none of these; and I could sense she did not want to battle me. Rather, she was observing me to see what I was, and what armor my body might have, as she also calculated a strategy of defense, should I want to attack her. I could tell she paid special attention to my difference. She seemed to study my different colored feathers, and my wings shape and texture. But she especially took notice of the sharp talons on my wings, my blue body, and my unusual internal glow of orange! I could sense she had then decided she did not wish to be in a battle with me, even though she was much larger than I. She was almost twice my size in length and width, so I too did not wish to battle her neither! I did not know what her strengths were, nor her abilities, so I kept my distance! After approximately fifteen minutes of observing one another, I heard a deep, thunderous, female voice in my head. *'What are you?'* It caught me by surprise, as a shock actually, for not only was it sudden, but it was powerful and a lot like thunder! I decided to answer her. I sent my thoughts to her. *'I am She, becoming Phoenix!'* I answered. She was quiet, still circling and studying me, trying to understand the meaning of my words. *'Phoenix?'* she asked. She paused in her circling, but only for a few seconds, thinking and observing me with a more scrutinous eye; then she continued her circling in her private circle, still maintaining a distance. *'What is this Phoenix?'* she asked. I too circle in my own small private circle, observing *her*. I thought before I spoke, deciding whether I should tell her anything else. She was so much more like myself than any other creature I had seen in all these hundreds of years of burning, and re-turning again to life here on Earth, that I decided to answer her. I also wanted to know who, and what, **she** was! So I spoke, in hopes I could discover if she and I had family ties and purpose. *'I do not know quite myself. The great Divine Mother, and Father, of all things tell me the Phoenix is what I am becoming; and for a purpose I am yet to be told of.'* She quietly and slowly continued circling; now moving closer to me to observe me further and more closely; seeming less concerned that I might be an aggressive creature she should fear and stay far from. I stayed where I was, this time not circling, so I could better observe her, and her intentions, preparing myself should she be intending to do battle! She had moved, covering half of the distance she had been, so to better observe me, yet was still more than eight times the length of my body away from me. When I stopped, she too stopped circling. She again spoke to me in our minds. *'Never seen I another like me, nor even similar to me. I have traveled these skies for over a hundred years, still, never have I come across a sister! Be you sister?'* she asked of me. *'I do not know, but we do resemble. What are you?'* I asked. *'I know not. Once I was not, then I was. I've always known aloneness. Others like me I've never found. I have seen my reflection in a large body of water, in the area where I awoke to, but other than that, another like I, I have never seen… I go to a lake when*

I feel too lonely, and there I see my own image and imagine it is not I, but a sister, and I am no longer alone...' I felt her pain of loneliness, and my Spirit and Soul went out to her! I could identify with her pain, and her loneliness. I hoped almost desperately, that we were blood sisters; and if not, I hoped me could be sisters in Spirit and purpose! *'Never?'* I asked, *'Never have you a recall of even a mother?' 'Not ever... no, never have I.* she said, and added, *Never have I known myself nor the how of my being. I only recall a great deafening noise and the bright electrical flash of light that followed. There I began. I looked up from the sea I rose up from, to the dark sky, searching for the source of the flash of electrical light that had struck Earth and Sea; its results sizzling, and fiery; delivering me! I rose up from the Earth, beneath the Sea, still looking upwards, but only seeing darkness... Then droplets of water fell gently from the heavens, baptizing me in purity, and coolness; helping to lower my body's fiery heat. And a gentle wind came, removing the smoke and steam off my body and into a stream of smoky mist! My body and I had been deposited to Earth and Sea by that which I now know as: lighting... and its voice is called Thunder...'*

So I learned that the Thunderbird-She was also from Earth, heat, fire and light, as was I; and even though she was also birth from the sea and Earth, she still was fire, heat and light... and so, we became sisters for one another! Alone no more.... I learn o, and from her; and she learned of, and from me! She would, however, at times, go her own way in her search for her purpose, and I would go wherever my instincts lead me; practicing and learning what I needed to experience, learn, and master for my Divine purpose and mission. I wanted to tell her what I had learned all those hundreds of years here, and from our Eternal Creators of life, but I had to ask permission first from them: the Divine Ones that know all things! I could not interfere with the Divine's will, or the will of those on Earth.! I believed however, in the innate core of me, that The Thunderbird-She also was created for a higher purpose by the

Divine. I suspected this because of the story she told me of the way she was created. She was an enigma! I knew *then* our paths were starcrossed; Divine intervened; and our paths would continue to cross and *always* meet! We were indeed Sisters of Spirit, and I knew then, somehow, for some reason, our destiny was also a Soul meeting, chosen, and set by the Supreme Divine...and one day we would know why...

We traveled together for many years before we came across the two Dragons, who, it seemed, traveled always together. It turned out they were twins, brother and sister, also seeking others of their kind! Since we were three species, not like any other, and not finding others like ourselves, we all soon became friends. The Dragons could exhale flames if they needed to. So they too were of the fire. In the fireheat, and the light, we were related. The fire however was not only my first beginning as the creature I was becoming, but it was also my ending as well as my beginning, in my becoming more! I had to, and had been, experiencing fire and my burning; and learning from it! So I knew it was possible for it to grow out of proportion, and maybe even reach out to consume my companions and others, in its fiery attempt to purify. I then also knew they too would have to go through the lessons and trials of the fiery red ray frequencies, if they were indeed Chosen Ones of the Divine All. By their being rare and having great abilities, I realized they too, were indeed chosen to serve the Divine, so to aid 'mankind'. Over the years we had our conflicts, even battles, but remained friends and together. And although I never seen them burn up, I knew they too somehow were being taught of the color ray spectrums of this world...

A few times, over the many years, I was drawn to the east, and towards Atlantis! I did not know why at the time I was feeling such a strong drive to head in that direction. The Thunderbird and Dragons went with me. We were now family. A strange and fearsome sight we must have been, seen flying together! We flew close to Atlantis, then over it! The people, along with the city, had expanded. All came out to watch us, after a loud sound from the city was given! Different loud sounding horns brought them all together; each sound meaning something different. I do believe some of the people were frightened of us; for when the Dragons began to show off, exhaling fire up towards the sky, they huddled back, about to bolt for indoor cover! This was the Dragon's way of also letting them know they had a power of their own mastered as well, and it would be in the Atlaneans' best interest if they do not **ever** attempt to try anything with us! My companions had heard my story about what the Atlantean Geneticists and Scientists had done, and were most probably *still* doing; plus they'd had their own experience with them; and, it still angered them! Flashes of memories suddenly began to come flooding back to me, releasing something in me that was not intentional, but rather impulsive! I then screamed out in the anger, bitterness, and the rage that was beginning to surface! I vented all those heated emotions towards the Scientists, Geneticists, and their Rulers! They of course only heard my loud and powerful screams and squawks. My thoughts, emotions, and visions of pass memories were empowered in my voice, empowering my actions! I screamed out to them, *'You, of the outer circle of life, of the realms of darkness, sacrificing the light, should know the power and fury of the water and its purification, least you learn of the power of the fire!'* I wanted to send the sea and the rain down upon them, but only enough to frighten them! The male Dragon asked of me, *'You wish them to burn?'* I quickly answered, *'Yes!'* but before I could complete that sentence, he shot out a flame of fire to the city, and his sister did the same soon after, following his lead! *'NO!'* I shouted to them. *'STOP! I did not mean for them to literally burn by fire!'* and I shoved the male Dragon away, to displace his second aim on the city! The female, confused, ceased the sending of fire from her mouth; and the brother, not understanding my actions either, also ceased. I quickly turned to the

Thunderbird, *'Bring your rain! Drown out the fires!'* The male Dragon asked me in a voice of concern, *'Did you not say you wished they would burn?'* Meanwhile the Thunderbird moved further away from the fire and flapped her massive wings creating no wind but thunder! Then she called out, sounding like continuous thunder, invoking the Spirits of the clouds to release their waters! While she was doing this, I answered the Dragon, as I headed for the ocean to gulp up water, and deposited it over the fires! *'Come, help gather water!'* I loudly yelled out to the Dragons. *'To answer your question; yes, but I had not finished with what I was trying to say to you! I meant that I wish they would burn up the toxins on their Soul and Spirit, and be reborn to a more pure entity! In my anger, and its voice, I was misunderstood. It is now* **my** *lesson, and,* **my** *price to pay...'* The Dragons and I swept up water to pour upon the flaming city, while the Thunderbird commanded the rain! It was not long before the fire was put out; but as it burned, the people screamed from fear and horrendous pain. Much of the city had burned, and many lives were destroyed. Since the city was made of mostly stone, in the forms of marble, ivory, and granite, casted with brass, copper, silver and gold, much survived the fire! But those metals caught in the fire were melted, running together, then cooling and hardening, creating strange structures, sealing up some passages into and out of the buildings. *'I did not mean harm...I did not mean the physical fire...'* I said softly out loud to myself as I was filled with shock, staring out at the damage being done. My companions looked at me saddened. *'I am sorry...'* the brother Dragon said to me. *'Sorry am I too...so sorry...'* the sister Dragon said. The Thunderbird-She looked at me with knowing and compassionate eyes. Those innocents: those not guilty of the cruelty done to me, my parents, and all the others that were harmed, had lost their lives, along with their home, painfully so, because I did not **think** before I spoke, but rather, I allowed anger and resentment to overtake my emotions, voice, and my thoughts as well. I had also wished harm, and spoken harm to them; casting my words, emotions, and vision forth;

invoking and creating that which I spoke! I again had failed to master my thoughts, words and emotions. I had, through my many life times, raised my energy, and my knowledge, higher than the mundane, and most of those who then living on this planet; thereby I was capable of manifesting things into existence quicker than most. I then was responsible not just because of my saying the word yes to the Dragons, but because of my other words that were accompanied with hateful visions, undisciplined anger, and thoughts! I had failed what I had been working towards achieving in my evolution. Yet, I also knew that I would be given more chances, before I burned, because my intentions were not to destroy and harm. I also knew, however, I had to bring out of me, and draw upon, the empathy within myself so to want to, and be able to, counter-act it and balance it, with compassion and gentleness; for them and life in all its forms.

We four flew quickly away from the city after we had doused out the fires. I lingered behind looking down at the people and the city. I tried to send them my thoughts of regret; but what had been done to them was too much, they were full of rage and sorrow; this would live on in their minds for as long as they walked the Earth... The Dragons and the Thunderbird would never be forgotten. *I* would never be forgotten. But forgotten I wanted to be, for I would be remembered not for what I didn't want, nor wished to happen, but rather for what **had** happened...

My companions and I stayed together for many years exploring the world. They did not burn as I did, but they were also going through the lessons of learning and mastering the many paths of life; plus learning about themselves and their place in it. There were times we were hunted, and times where we rebelled and allowed our anger and our fires to strike back at our adversaries. We created many deaths, and many tried to create ours…

During the many years of our travels, I began to have flashes of Déjà vu, with bits of images and feelings stirring and flashing in my mind. They were images from memories of a time long ago; images of my parents and family! It had been close to two hundred Earth years since I last saw them. I had not remembered them, except for a few moments in pass life times, and during my returns to Earth. I only remembered them entirely and lastingly when I was returned to the other side, the world of Spirit! But I was now, during my time spending with my new family: the Dragons and the Thunderbird, beginning to recall my Earth parents and family completely; feeling a great urgency to locate them! This was just before I burned…

I had burned during the time of another emotional outburst of uncontrollable rage. My three companions and I were sitting quietly upon the ground. We had feasted upon some white woolly creatures that are known to you today as sheep. They had been grazing on grass in a meadow close to a farm house. There were at least fifty of them. My companions and I were hungry, and had been hunting for a long time for food. The first we had come upon were these white wool four legged creatures. We had never seen anything like them before! We were in another country far from the land where we had first met. We had to eat, and so when we saw them we dove down to capture some, and take them where we could eat in peace. I had told the Dragons that they should not use their fire for it would kill more than we could eat for now, and it would be best to have fresh meat to eat now and later, by only killing several each. There were other good reasons for this, but I won't go into that now. We had captured and killed three each. We had carried them off to a clearing where we quickly and mercifully ended their life and then devoured them! We had finished our meal and were resting for several hours, growing drowsy, when there was a sudden bursting of humans coming through the bushes with guns, pitch forks and other instruments of destruction! There must have been fifteen male humans, full of anger and determination, coming at us to take our lives! We had taken the lives of their livestock and so they wanted to take ours! At the time we did not realize that those white woolly creatures were property of anyone or anything! We soon learned that the humans did not always hunt for their meals, but captured and contained their food alive for future use.

The humans rushed on to us, foolish and brave! They shot their guns of 'thunder', and succeeded in injuring the female Dragon! They had shot her in her left shoulder. This enraged the other Dragon and I! The Thunderbird, I could tell, was also angered, but was trying to calculate her best attack strategy. While I stood facing our attackers, she flew up high over them! The male Dragon had moved protectively in front of his wounded sister, and at the same moment the Thunderbird-She flew upwards! The angered male Dragon let loose his fire on those that had advanced! The humans who had not advanced began to turn to run, while those caught in the flames screamed and melted; but the Thunderbird was already descending to return the attack! She flew down, grasping one of the men with her talons, flying higher up to drop him, while I too had flew over to those who were retreating! I grabbed one and flew up high, carrying him high enough that when I dropped him he would be no more! The Thunderbird-She was returning to the Dragons, allowing the other three to run free. But I did not stop! I went after another one, capturing him in my beak this time, so enraged was I! I bite him hard in the side and his abdomen at the same time! He screamed louder than all the others, and I felt a bit of satisfaction and delight over it! I was about to go after the other two; for my rage had found delight, and was like a demanding child, wanting what it wanted, with no regards of the consequences or right or wrong of it! My rage behaved like a selfish demanding beast, gone amuck! The Dragons too wanted to fight! The female could not yet fly, due to her wound; but the male, seeing that there was no longer a threat to the female, took flight to join me in our killing frenzy! The Thunderbird-She, who had somehow managed to keep her rage under control, flew in front of us, quicker than I had ever seen her fly, startling us! She shouted out to us, *'STOP! Stop NOW! Let them go to warn others to leave us be. Can't you see this is the best way?'* We tried to push pass her, but she spread her large, powerful wings wide! *'Release your rage!'* She demanded! *'**You** are the master, not your anger!'* The male Dragon slowed, but puffed frustrated smoke; snorting and panting, as he struggled for control over the emotions that battled within him for release! He began to gain control over the rage, and his breathing softened and deepened. He began to relax, allowing his senses and his mind to function normally. But I did not! Rather, I allowed my rage to live! I pushed angrily pass the Thunderbird's large wings! She turned, following me, while the Dragon looked on in surprise! Just as I would have flew down to capture one of the terrified men, I suddenly combusted and began to flame up! I then realized I had allowed ***again*** my actions and emotions to master me! I looked to my friends, voicing in my mind my farewell. *'You were right Thunderbird, I was wrong! You and the Dragons have mastered faster than I, and I regret it; and I regret that I now must leave you. I hope when I return again, you shall still be, and we will meet again...Farewell, Dear friends...'* I remember the looks upon their faces; the looks of amazement, sorrow, and helplessness to help me. The flames grew higher, but I kept my eyes upon my friends, my heart saddened, as I tried to imprint them forever in my memory in hopes I'd never forget them; and also in hopes those memories would come forth in my consciousness when I would again return to the next Earth-life-time. Before I was totally consumed by the fire, my family of friends had said to me, in a sorrowful desperate voice, *'We want to help, but we don't know how!'* When I knew I was only seconds away from being totally consumed, and had already said my farewell, they had cried out, *'We will never forget you! You are our friend for all time! Farewell sister...till we meet again...let us meet again...'*

I then returned to a higher place of learning, but not to the higher place I last had been. I had to rest again, and then when awakened, begin again in the red and orange ray's dimensions of learning. The Forever One, the Supreme Creator/s, said to me, *'It is easy to get lost in uncertainties. Through your life times you have been experiencing those thoughts and emotions of uncertainties. You are still in the first stages of moving into the higher rays, and so you must face uncertainties and make a decision: whether you wish to keep advancing your light and higher ascension, or to slow it down and play longer in the dimension of illusions of separation, duality and matter; reducing your learning experiences; thus experience more out of sync energy and the chaos it creates! All of your personal being of light has been increasing by the higher frequencies you have raised your body, mind, and Spirit to, due to all the learning, experiencing, and your choosing to rise again and again to become a higher life form and giver to life! In your journey back to the light, the higher light, you will find darkness coming to greet you. The dark seeks the light, and it will follow you. It will come to you to be alchemized and to share its time of existence with you before it is alchemic. At those times, it, and things of matter too will be faced with uncertainties and fears, moving toward your light, yet moving away again; not yet ready to join with the light, blending with it, becoming one with it! It is then acting like a yo-yo, up and down; or pendulum, swinging back and forth; creating challenges and sometimes chaos; and then moving away, causing relief and peace; even great prosperity and joy! The more pleasant and joyful your experiences, the higher you vibrate! The higher you vibrate, the more you draw its counterpart, so the more challenges you will have brought to you to allow you to choose again! And if your choice is to move upwards again in vibration and knowledge of the light and its wisdom, you will then be given the challenges that are for you personally to go through and learn, and thus, grow in the light to move into the higher light! These challenges are practice. They are challenges of learning to empathize and alchemy: the blending of both counter-parts together to bring out the gifts of balance to you and the world, creating synchronicity; having the light and the dark work* **together** *to* *achieve true life and all it offers! You and everyone, need to learn to stay calm, grateful, humble, and assured! Seek the gift these challenges bring, and then calmly and gratefully allow the disturbances to move away, resisting them not. This then will also bring about understanding, knowledge, and eventually, wisdom, in its appliance, usage, and acceptance; and also in its and your creating! Even though the counter-parts seek one another, one can learn to control their negative influences and how they affect one and another. By calming one's emotions and thoughts, neutralizing them; not allowing them, nor fear, to rule you, one will be able to grasp more quickly the reasons for the chaos, and the lessons of Divine light, and sound, that one is to learn. Then the chaos will neutralize and turn to the up-swing of its counterpart and you shall experience peace, joy, and your positive needs and desires! The world you are becoming your* **true** *self in, known to its inhabitants as, Earth, (and so it is known by that name to us as well), is a dimensional holographic world with the illusionary sense of separation from one another, all things, and me, and all I create! It is a world of illusion....a hologram that was allowed to be created to bring about individualities and diversities. This experience also offers aspects of me; parts of me; to observe, experience, explore, play, create, and to will new things into being; my learning more of and about what I have been creating and will put into motion; so that I, and those,(my) Individualized selves, will one day know what to alter, keep, or add, to better perfect my creations! Earth is then yours, and others, simplified, yet expansive education! It is yours, and all others', playground and prep-higher schooling; allowing all of you to become more like me, whom you came forth from, and are a part of! I dwell within you, and within* **all** *I create!* **I am** *all creation! All creation is* **me!** *This is why you are learning to control your awareness; your five senses; your emotions; thoughts; actions; will; and your words! Words are creation! Sound is creation and creating! Thoughts and emotions are creation! Create, for I create! Move, for I move! Sing, for I sing, and* **all life** *sings with you! Dance, for I, and all life, dances! Beware* *of your actions, and the words you chose, think and say! Be aware of what you wish and will to be; for **all life responses**! And all life has a reaction, and a voice, with a result…*

'You must stay calm and raise your vibrations throughout all *the dark-like times: the challenges, the synchronizing of polarities, and any chaos; for it will calm the fury of the darker times and make you neutral, as if invisible or free floating and above it. You shall eventually learn how to balance your polarities when the law of compensation returns to you after each pendulum-like 'up-swing' or 'down swing' you feel and experience. You will eventually learn how to raise your polarity, your vibration, and your ego, high enough to rise up over the dis-harmonies, conflicts, and un-pleasantries! You do this with love, joy, and trust in a higher power living within you, and available to all; extending into ecstasy, with the intention of, and for, good for all!*

'Have fun and laughter, yes! And enjoy life and beauty, for they bring about pleasant changes; but when the 'teachers of challenges' are drawing close, coming in multiples, and over-whelming you, go within, to your still place! Gather and feel the peace, and my presence there. Feel the beauty and serenity there! Smile and feel joy, envisioning me lovingly holding your hand as that circle of life's compensations begins to spiral counter-clock-wise with the polarity of lessons it brings; seeming to pull you down into a dark place! But it cannot take you forever down and under, for I hold you from above, vibrating my highest love! Then see what good, and what lessons, you could gain and learn from the challenges! When you have meditated on that, and grasped the positive of it, see the spiral spinning back the other way, clock-wise, lifting you up out of that swirling darkness that feels like it's over taking you and trying to suck you in! See it spinning clock-wise, lifting you to the brighter light of day; a re-birth, that gathers more love, enlightenment, strength, peace, and awareness; and all things of beauty! Be still in feelings of safety, happy appreciation, and calmness; quietening your

mind for a while. Then again seek in your mind, and your heart of hearts, with gratitude, your Over-Soul, for the understanding of **why** the challenges have visited you at this time. Ask your Over-Soul and me: the **true** Creator/Higher Power, how you can make the unpleasant situation/s, the challenge/s, serve towards good for you and for **all** life. And how the challenges can strengthen, enlighten, teach, and assist you, in helping yourself and Creation. Then smile and be grateful, offering your troubles to me to be transmuted and dispersed into light; gifting that light to all creation! You, like others, will occasionally slip up, and feel, at times, over-whelmed by the quickening of the so often visits from the challengers. But all lapses, all shortcomings are forgiven! When one misses the mark, I always forgive to allow each one another chance. I then deliver a repeated lesson. It is only when a life form is filled with selfish, and greedy toxins, that serve only its self, yet while doing so harms the life-form it occupies, or harms others, in some destructive poisoning way, having no desire to change; thus accumulating more than it willingly will, or can, dispel, that I must recycle it! Those damaging toxins are due to selfish serving of the self; fear of losing the self; and not desiring to seek, nor follow, the purpose for **all** life, and all that occurs; has occurred; and is meant to occur, for all the reasons life was created. The life force which is recycled, still yet lives; for life essence is; was; and always shall be! It is forever pure and **never** destroyed! It is only changed; separating the not needed from the needed, moving again into what those on Earth call: Love/light! Yours, and all that are in existence, struggles and stumbles are not only one's learning, but also creation's learning and becoming; for all are a part of the whole of creation! So, forgive yourself; and when you ask forgiveness you are not only asking **me** for forgiveness, but you are also asking your Soul and your Spirit to forgive you, and all of creation to forgive you, and free you from the grasp/bondage of the 'challengers', and the bonds of the 'playground yo-yo' effect that wants you to always struggle, then play; and then struggle and play again; mindlessly, and without truth; staying unaware of truth, and not *growing more enlightened! This yo-yo affect is so not to just hold one dependent and addictive to that state of illusion, but to allow one choices; creating one's experiences of both sides of creation and creating on Earth, and later, a wise creator and partner of all creation! Life is meant to be fun, and playing with enjoyment is both good and required. But constant 'blind, mindless', and careless fun, without awareness of Spirit, Soul, and its effects on all life, and what should be sought and learned of them, their purpose, and desires, can become unhealthy, additive, selfish, and stagnated habits and thinking, if the Spirit and Soul are **not** also engaged in the fun and play. Fun and playing then can sometimes mislead you, delaying you, if it, and your Spirit disconnects from your Soul, and then self-pleasure and self-service for only the individual self becomes the only things one does or desires to do and obtain! Life can be additive as well; and it is meant to be, but with a higher purpose and goal for the 'bigger picture'; which means, the **whole** of creation, not just the individual self/s! It is the loving, unselfish discipline, and blending of life, others, and fun/play, you are created to do, experience, learn, and then master through the alchemy! For you, my beloved Phoenix, and also all my beloved humans, and all my creations, are Spirits connected to a Soul! My humans are Spirits having a human experience: experiences of being human! You and they are potential master Alchemists; Alchemists of the joining of the Spirit with matter and human emotions; joining them and the self with the Soul! All are connected to the one main Soul atom and source of life: Me! You are meant to 'awaken' to that truth.*

*'You, Zep-Tii-Us-She-ia, are to become a universal life master, guardian of the universe, and a messenger of truth, for me; and you are quickly doing so with your rapid re-births. A Master Spirit is aware and knowledgeable. S/he can will things to be with a **clear and wise** mind. If not s/he remains a cloudy, confused, unaware, and self-centered mind! A master of a particular thing or subject is one who has earned, through experiences of trial and error, thus gained a second nature of understanding,*

*knowledge, and wisdom; doing all s/he does with calm understanding, knowing, trust, empathy, respect, consideration, compassion, and confidence! To be a master, you would be, therefore, skilled, wise, and at one with the things you have mastered. Your skills would become innate and at one with you. You become it, it becomes you! You then can maintain, easier and quicker, the synchronicity of the world you live in; and then all you need comes to you; unnecessary fear removed! The goal of achieving mastery of body, mind, matter, and the five senses, so to achieve Spirit perfection and Soul purpose, is accomplished by being a master that **calmly** flows like a stream of water in* all of *something and everything. Being a master in creative willing and un-willing: a master and partner with the Supreme Creator in co-creating; is doing it with consideration of* **all** *it may affect; and doing it with the goal of flowing and ebbing, peacefully, back again, to and with, the harmonious Supreme and Original Source-Substance of all things, referred to as, the One True God: Mother-Father God…Me! This is life's purpose! The* **true** *master has learned the art of perfecting one or more skills, but with compassion, love, self-control, and good judgment! S/he has learned to stay calm and in good faith, controlling their emotions, thoughts, words, and actions, doing and saying all with love, compassion, empathy, and confidence, while including their ego, but taming it! The master is mindful of what s/he does, doesn't do, says, doesn't say, thinks, and creates! S/he also considers the consequences of his/her words, thoughts, and actions, and what effects they have on others, self, and on the world as a whole.*

'You, Tii-Us-She, my Phoenix and my delight, have desired for many life times, to see your Earth biological family again. Tii-Us, Dear Phoenix…they are no longer living on the Earth plane… Many hundreds of Earth years have passed since you last seen them. They are now in an-other dimension other than Earth. I will take you there, for you have longed for so long. to be with family; and your heart has been faithful and true to my purpose and my desire. My Desire for you to become what I want from you

has been also your desire. Know, Dear one, that wherever love has lived; love can live again! Whenever two or more experience love, they have created love, they then are adding love not only to one another but also to the etheric field around them! And it expands, adding love to the world; creating multi-colored emotional and Soul energy that can again be re-generated, bringing back those moments, bringing back those that were loved! Come, Tii-Us; come. Come, and greet your family…' I was then taken to one dimension higher; and there my family was, *all of them*, and some extra family members as well! My brothers and sisters had found mates on Earth, since I had last seen them, and now had children of their own! And while on Earth, those children also had children, who also had children, who had children! And so the gene pool had continued! There were thirteen generations there, in that Spirit world, and I met every one of them! I truly was in my paradise! My joy was boundless! And they greeted me the same! The Eternal One/s told me that after the thirteenth generation they were rendered sterile because the Eternal Creator/s did not want certain traits to be bred out; plus the Creator/s did not want my parents and their generations to remain on Earth any longer, so they returned them to the Spirit world! The Eternal Creator: male and female aspects as One, wanted only a certain number of my family's kind to exist on Earth, and for only a certain amount of time. There were after that, no more on Earth like them. Now they are all removed, except for the occasional visits of one of them or me. They all now dwell in a higher abode to create and share there, their vibrations of a higher order, and then be sent to other worlds to aid, adding their light frequency to raise the life forms into awareness of their true self and purpose. This is so to work in harmonious synchronicity with the rest of the universe!

During my visit with my family, I had wanted to explained to my parents and my siblings, whom I had met while on Earth, why I had not returned to them again as I had promised I would when I again would returned to that planet; but, they already knew why…

I was allowed to spend with them, what would be considered by Earth's measurement of time, to be forty-nine years. After that I was told I had to go back to Earth and learn more of *all* the rays and their influences so I could eventually obtain my highest potential, and thus complete and continue on my journey; following my destiny of becoming the Rainbow Phoenix: Messenger, Guardian, and Assistant to and for the Creator/s of *all* things! After the forty-nine years I spent with my family in paradise, I was again put to 'sleep' in the chamber of no-thoughts to again, after I had completed my rest, be re-awaken to meditate upon all I had chosen over my life times; all my experiences and reactions; what I had learned; and what I wanted to keep. And, that which I needed to give away to the Divine Purging 'Fire' to be transmuted into a higher, more brilliant light for the universe, to raise my frequency to enable me to rise to a higher dimension/heaven so to be able to approach the Creator! This purging 'fire' I would need to go through every time I entered the Spirit World! And then again be purged; but a more complete, intense, and personal, purging: one to remove those lower vibrations, thought forms, and impurities, that I had created or picked up while on Earth; and one that would let me see my choices, and feel the effects that they had on me, on others, and on the world as a whole! I would shed, as if a burning, due to the spiritual pain of knowing and feeling the effects my words and actions had on others, all the debris of impurities and inverted love I had collected from mine and other's negative thought forms/vibrations and deeds! This would happen after I had spoken to the Eternal Supreme: the True One Mother-Father-Life-Source-Creator. After the purging, I would enter the chamber of no-thoughts to rest before I was to again experience a heavenly state there in that Spirit dimension of learning and practicing; and before returning to the Earth Plane. So each time before I returned to Earth, I felt the discomforts and griefs of the 'fire' that purges, and I saw and felt the effects of what I said and did; and I saw and felt how others felt, and what effect their words had, along with what I created by my thoughts, words, actions, deeds, and emotions! Each time, after that, I'd be allowed to experience the paradise there in the higher abode; then I was again sent back to Earth! I was to experience again, another color, or the same color, and experience the imbalances that were a kind of hell, until I learned it/them well and could master and control their influences, earning another colored feather or two; and along with it, earning a higher frequency of light and awareness of myself, of life, others, and of all aspects and effects of in-sync and not in-synced energies and chaos! As well as that of love...and, I was learning more about our Creator of all things...

After my time with my family in the world of Spirit, I was returned to Earth to learn of the color blue, which my body became, and the dominating counter-part color, the internal glow of orange. I burned six more times after that, before I was to go on to learn of the glowing inner blue in its dominating color ray, with its counter-part orange as the lesser influential body color. With the internal color blue I learned about creating and destroying; changing and re-creating. I learned what and how changes and chaos came to be, and their purpose! I learned of peace and the necessity of disruption so to keep moving and expanding creation. I also learned about heaven as well as hell: as in, a heaven of experiences of great joy and pleasure; and a hell of experiences of great sorrow and misery! I had to learn that words, thoughts, and emotions can command illusions, seeming real. In the blue light I had to especially learn of the power of words, the will, and manifesting! Since blue, on the spectrum scale, lay between the colors, green and indigo, I had to also learn how those colors that were next to blue could affect it and the power of the blue will in creating and manifesting things into this world of illusions, seeming real: from the void of the unmanifest, which is surrounded by, and gets its power from, **the *true* real** in the heavens!

Green of heart made the blue will more desiring and wanting. Indigo of the knowing, and connection with Soul and the Spirit world, made the blue of will more believable and true, giving it more real to life! I also had to earn wisdom by experiencing not only the counter-parts of each color, but also how they influence one another, and *everything*! I had to learn all the colors' gifts and their power control. It took many Earth years to learn those things; and each time I accumulated too many negative thought forms, growing too weary to process, and to set free to be transmuted, it meant I needed to rest and grow spiritually stronger. It was then I *was* set to flames so to burn them off! I next, would then go before the Supreme One/s. I eventually, each time, after returning to the Spiritual World,

Be returned again to Earth so to practice what I had learned from that previously life, as well as learn what I had practiced and learned in the higher abode of the Spirit World of learning! I was given free will, and therefore, allowed to choose whether I wanted to master my five senses, along with their temptations, or to merely play longer with them on Earth, experiencing full force, the back-lash of out-of-order; along with play, and fun; which is then moved forward, full circle, returning back again into disorder, confusion, and chaos; then back again to balance and pleasure, and order; and then both cycles repeating over and over again and again: the experiencing of both Heaven and Hell on Earth!

When the internal glow of blue would switch back down the color scale to the color spectrum of green, I would have to also learn of the Soul-Heart and the Earth, along with the natural healing they offered. I would then learn to connect to them and the universal light, so to retain and call forth healing and perfect balance; order; and communication, in, and with, my body and its cells, and also with other life forms! I also learned of the pure, more powerful effects of the Earth's energy when connected fully with her and the Divine Light! My inner glow, and body, would change colors as well during these times. When I was learning of the green ray, and all its love and healing, I would change to red of the body, then red internal, and learn of the life force, and the passionate red 'fire 'of energy, anger, passion, and desire; along with all that it influenced, or it was influenced by! When I would glow pink I would experience red along with all the multiple lights that blended peacefully into each other, creating the pure white light of unconditional love for others and self. Sometimes I lost control of all I had learned to control; along with my emotions, my thoughts, and my actions! At other times, I would 'tame' them, and then understand all they had to offer, and teach me! Other times I would become frustrated, not caring if I tamed or controlled them, or if I allowed them to run free and out of control!

With the blue ray I also learned of the power of wishes and desires, and the positive and the negative side of creation! I learned how I could create life experiences with words and thoughts, good and not so good. I'd then experience them and be drawn back into the down side or the up side of whatever I'd given into. When I went into the blue-indigo inner glow, and the body color of peach, I'd learn more about the mind and the super-conscious, and how to communicate with my Spirit and Soul. I would also learn how to communicate with other species on Earth, and with those species on other planes of existence! I'd glow indigo, and my body would turn the color peach! When I glowed violet, my body would turn the color yellow! I would then know many things, feeling more love for creation and for the Divine that creates all things! At those times I would begin to gain more communication with the Eternal One/s, the Divine Creator/s of all things, and with the Hierarchy of higher dimensions! I would then, at that time, glow a golden color, and my body would become violet-gold, emitting white light all around me! It was then that I could choose to transcend to, and remain, in the higher dimensions of tranquility, love, and bliss! Many times I would transport myself there for a time. When I transcended there, I joyfully existed, doing whatever the Eternal One/s instructed me to do; going wherever they willed me to go, yet doing also whatever I desired from the goodness of my Soul! This I had earned. I was given the choice to return to Earth; stay there and do the Original One of All's work for that world, or go to another planet to go through their energy rays and help those of that world. I was also told that I still needed to learn more about the violet ray's influence on Earth and its inhabitants; that is, if I decided to go on to assist Earth, mankind, and all living upon her; thereby fulfilling the Supreme Divine One/s purpose and desire for me, Earth, and humankind! I was then told that Earth's energies effects not only her but all her other worlds above her; and also the entire universe! So if I chose to return to Earth until I had mastered and earned the gift of power to help her and hers from the heaven places, I would be helping not only all of Earth, but also the Creator of all life, and all life that has been created so far in **all** the universes… in all of creation… I was also told that it meant I would help make it possible for the universes to expand and continue on without a great destruction to all that was thus created so far, and all which was constantly being created. So… I chose to return to Earth…

When I returned to Earth, Atlantis was warring with several different civilizations…one being Lemuria: Mu, which stood for mother in their language. The Lemurians were also etheric beings…. I ventured far from their battles to another part of the world, exploring new things and new places. In spite of my distancing, I was soon lead, by the Supreme Source of All, to others: human, animal and reptile, and a variety of other species, to experience conflicts and to test my emotions before I was to again experience the color of the violet ray. I had strange things happening to me, and seen strange occurrence, and happenings in, and to, others. Many creatures would seem to be magnetically drawn to me, and were friendly, seeming to like me. Then, after a time, they seemed to change towards me, and become hostile and hateful; turning away from me, canceling me out as their friend and companion; becoming adversaries instead; attempting to torture me in some form; striking out at me for reasons I did not understand, nor seem to have a reason for! I began to feel all alone and an outcast! No place, nor no one, others, the world, and its events, did I seem to be a part of. I had a great heaviness come over me that darken life and my will, and desire to exist. I thought of burning and refusing to exist anywhere, no matter what the Supreme All would say! I wished for my death in the truest sense of that word! I wanted to not exist! I now knew darkness in its most powerful form of isolation and aloneness...separation from the God of all creation, as well as light, and in it, I sunk deep inside myself...I began, in the truest form of the words, to finally know my-Self....While I learned of my lower self, I also learned of my higher Self. This was the **true** One-Self, of all things, which all is, and all is part of, and connected to…

With the indigo and violet color rays I learned how to be happy and content with myself, and content alone, with myself. But I was never really alone, for I was connected and apart of **all things**, which included the Divine Supreme, the Creating Life Force... While I learned the things of the heart of hearts, the Soul, I learned of agape love, unconditional! I learned of its sadness and its joys, and their effects upon the body, and the mind, and even upon one's actions! And its effects on other people and things! I learned to love my biological and my universal family more, and to forgive more. I learned to love more than myself, yet love myself. In the universal love I learned to love the Earth and all upon her, and all that I could see with my Earth eyes, and all I could not see, yet existed somewhere, some place, in some world, and in some time, an***d even beyon***d time…

When I would internally glow blue-green and my body was red-orange, I experienced the results of my manifestations when done with and also without fully thinking it through, and not giving it a lot of consideration; nor considering the responsibilities of my will-creating, and what those results were, and what I said, did, thought, and wished, would become, and bring forth! I had to learn to calm the senses, clear and still my mind, keeping a 'single eye' upon the good and beauty of the Eternal One/s wishes and purpose that I was intended for, and allowed to exist to become! I had to come willingly from the place of love. When I would gained the indigo color again, I'd developed more awareness of other worlds within worlds, occupying the same space as I, others, and the Earth; and yet, invisible to my and other's Earthen eyes' vibrational seeing! My inner glow would be at that time, indigo; and my body would go from the color of peach to violet, even yellow, depending upon what I had successfully accomplished; or what I was to combined with the indigo or violet ray, so to learn of its affects, powers, and gifts, when combined with the other color rays attributes and influences! With all those color spectrums I learned the consequences of my thoughts, and choices! I could also know others emotions and thoughts; including their thoughts and emotions towards me! With the indigo and violet rays I had to learn to face my ego again, and also learn how to tune out all the static of whispers and words I'd sensed or even heard! With these ray's experiences, I had to face my insecurities and my 'power-trips' where I'd feel, sometimes, superior to others, or less than; thus I had to face and experience the consuming of myself again, creating a Divine 'Fire' that would 'burn' me up in the indigo and the violet flame, as they burned up all those impure thought forms and the collected negative influential energies from my experiences on Earth! By this time I was taking to building a nest in the sacred willow tree before I was to burn; for I also now initiated my own 'burning'. I now knew when I was to let go and be consumed, and what I was letting go of and being released from; rising, spiraling, upward, to the high abode to join with the Creator/Supreme!

ஓ ஓஓ ஓஓ ஓஓஓ ஓஓ ஓஓ ஓ

When I built my nest, I'd first collect sweet spices, myrrh, and other fragrant herbs. This was to be my nest! Then I would start my fire, beginning at the tail. My tail would vibrate, igniting first to set my nest to flames! Then quickly the flames would flare up, all around me, quickly consuming me! I no longer felt pain from this, that I now knew was a blessing, not just for me, but for **all** creations! I went out singing, for I had gained great knowledge and understanding of why things were as they were, such as my burnings. My songs then became songs of joy that healed all those who heard them! In my Earthen body, I would usually sing when I was near water, and early in the morning, at first sunset! Water was also healing, and together with my singing, it not only intensified the healings, but it carried my songs a greater distance to heal what needed healed, and what needed put back into balance, and perfect order! Many people were now getting to know me, and so began their stories of me and my deeds: what they ***thought*** I was doing, and, what they ***thought*** I was... Some were correct... but many more than that were misinterpreted...

ஓ ஓஓ ஓ

Before I had arrived at that place of singing and knowing that enabled me to remove pain, and illness at will; and before I had at last, after many trials and burnings, mastered the indigo's influences and the gifts they offered, and was re-born again; I returned, re-born, flaming in the seventh ray! That ray was the violet ray! It flamed all around me and inside me! I had to 'dance' with it, blend with it, and respect it! My body was returned, glowing the color of the violet ray! But it would alter at first, between the colors of yellow, then peach and indigo. Later, as I worked with the violet ray, it would go back to red; orange; green; and blue; moving up the spectrum of the seven rays; pulsating those colors also within me; and doing so wilder then they had ever pulsed within me before! This violet flame, that I, at that time, stood re-born in, burned me stronger than all the other flames I had burned with! It tested me on all levels, and on all the ray's influences that I had graduated from. Yet never completely did I graduate from any of the rays. This violet color ray challenged me greater than all the other flaming colors before it! It did not allow me to know its gifts so easily. Although it was the purest, and more loving, and higher gifted, and gifting flame, it was also the most frightening, strongest, furious, and hardest of the rays to blend with, and to master its challenges! This was because it vibrated so high; thus, becoming a catalyst, removing impurities quicker from those who approached or entered that vibrating color than the other rays would do! And when one did arrive to enter that color spectrum, its light shining within them would catalyze them, others, and places as well, bringing forth one's worse fears, dark emotions, and memories! This was the 'Deliverer Ray', the highest color ray that is visible to the Earthen eye! This ray removes, and delivers, the last of the Earthen polluted energies,which have gone through the other six color rays, and now arrive at the higher visible color spectrum! This delivery ray delivers those pollutants to the next higher color ray spectrum which leads to the pure light of the Eternal One! There, they would be transmuted into the pure light of creation for more creation! The violet ray burning was a more detailed and complete burning of purification. Because of this it was frightening, bringing out my, and others, fears, furious, strong, and hard; because of its abilities and power to do what it was meant to do for the betterment of the Soul, in spite of the body's fears, misunderstandings and resistance! To approach the violet ray was to bring fear and great discomfort to that which is made of the lower vibrations, such as the body of matter, which the eternal light occupies on Earth at this, and even at, that time. The Soul and the Spirit, however, are drawn by the light, like a plant is, and so seeks the light, as if unconscious of the body's fears and its every attempt to stop it. But the fears, and the anger, and distrust of others, along with jealousies, paranoia, and other negative emotions, thoughts, and feelings, are all signs of this purification. It is not until the body has purged from those interfering toxins that it can be freed up to join with the violet light, and thus, be ascended to a higher plane of existence and knowing.

When I had finally, many years later, mastered the violet ray's teachings, I was able to live strictly on sunshine and dew. In fact I could even omit sunshine for I was now like the sun, thus sunshine I became, and sunshine I am, as well as am I fire! The dew refreshes me and keeps me hydrated as well as aides my healing powers. I could also now go to other dimensions and experience more of all that is. I had then reached paradox! A paradise of everything…a mind altering singularity! Yesterday became today. Today became yesterday; and all days became tomorrow, becoming present moment…all at the same time! All became NOW! Everything was and everything now IS! Paradox was weaving and moving, and shimmering like a mirror of water; ever changing, and yet remaining in the moment, real, and also reflecting illusions of self! Here I traveled in Spirit, Mind, and Soul to instant, universal **all** knowledge; **all** understanding; and **all** wisdom! All this was instant in its arriving, with a deep innate knowing; an always there knowing of all things! It was beyond anything I could remember when I was returned back to my flesh-clothed body, during my Earth lives; and it was more than I could completely remember, even when I'd return to the Spirit World to be prepared for my next Earth life experience! It was more than any memory could hold or retained in the Earth-dimensional light frequency, and even some of the dimensions a little higher than Earth's!

I saw worlds being birthed and then disappearing as if destroyed, yet like me, re-born again into more of itself! Born more into splendor and radiance! It is here where I really began; where my story of me, the Phoenix-born, really begins; for it is here that I became the Rainbow Phoenix, and thus, my real purpose began to be! A purpose meant to be shared with you;! And it was **then** that I was **truly** given the reason for my name and my purpose… *'You shall be named Tii-Us, after Atlantis: Atlanti-us, for you were designed there, and you were meant to return there as the Rainbow Phoenix to help that city and its people! Eventually, many years into the future, you will deliver for me a crucial message to their descendants and to **all** humans.'* The Creator had spoken those words to me, and also revealed so much more that I had ever wondered about! S/he told me why I had been prepared, and why I had to return again one day after I had mastered and learned and kept **consciously aware** of *all* I'd learned and experienced; along with compassion and wisdom! Then, after that, I was to return to Earth to deliver my story, along with its teachings and message, along with the Creator's message, to those who would listen and would share its warnings with others. I was now the "Rainbow Phoenix!" I had mastered not just once, but many times, **all the rays** of the seven major color spectrum; along with their spectrums of various hues of creation on Earth, including the Earth's Spiritual rays! This was the **true** law of mastery, the one the Atlanteans had forgotten, and at the time I was assembled by them, believed it had meant! The Atlanteans, at that time, even with all their advanced knowledge, had not yet again earned the gifts they'd lost of true knowledge, understanding, and wisdom! They had not re-learned, nor earned, the truth of mastery; therefore, they were **not true masters**!

So, after I had mastered all the rays, I, in agreement, was send back to Earth to be the symbolic and metaphoric symbol that represents, and would subconsciously be recognized by a laten innate knowing of the meaning of the symbolic message I represent. My Phoenix form was a symbol; an archetype; an encoded metaphoric memory implant that would, in time, reach *all* human forms, re-awakening their en-coded metaphoric and symbolic patterns that are encoded there; along with the Divine blueprints of **all creation,** that were placed in all creation, at the very beginning of creation. All life forms are filled with the mind and breathe (Spirit) of the Divine. This was done from the beginning of the Divine's first thoughts to form each life form. All creation then are the Divine Eternal Living Source/Force, and creating substance, in diversified expression, seeming separate, yet not.

Before I was sent here to deliver my story, its teachings, and the message I am to deliver to you and all mankind, I was again returned to Atlantis. It was hundreds of years after I was first formed by them. Because they had the long life DNA, especially those of the full blood line: those who came from the skies, some of those that were alive when my body was first created by their DNA, were still alive, and still in Atlantis! I was told by the All of All, that when I was able to keep consciously aware of all I'd learned and experienced from all the times I was returned to Earth; along with keeping compassion, understanding, and wisdom with what I had learned, I would then be ready to return to Earth on my Holy mission: to deliver my story, along with its teachings and messages to those who **would** listen and would share its warnings with others.

The same Geneticists, and Scientists, were still there when I again, hundreds of years later, flew again over Atlantis! The Atlanteans had rebuilt their city, which the Dragons had burnt; and it stood even more magnificent than before! They had brought more ivory to their city; dug more gold, silver, brass, and copper from the mountains, bringing them all to their island; and, their city showed it in bright sparkles reflecting off them from the sun light! It was so bright it was almost blinding! They also had the long neck dinosaurs pull more marble, alabaster, ivory and other large, heavy stones and materials, from the land, and through the waters, onto their shores of their city! Statues were carved from many of those; and from them more buildings with columns were made and erected! The white alabaster sparkled in the sun like white star dust, giving it a heavenly glow!

I rose up high, climbing upwards, my wings pulling the air currents downwards, grabbing them with my large wings like levers, to pull me up high in the morning sky! I climbed higher and higher to rise high over Atlantis! My long, pointy, reddish-purple, and rainbow speckled beak, was raised high towards the sky as I climbed upwards! I did not look down yet upon the city, but I knew they had spotted me, and were yet unsure what I was! Oh how surprised they must have been to zoom in on me with their high technical spying devices and see that I was in the form they had once created hundreds of years ago; looking also much like the bird that had traveled with the Thunderbird, and the Dragons who had set their city to blazing a hundred years ago, yet also looking much different, with a bright glow about me! I did not gloat in that. I simply was following my mission, and here to leave a mission statement. They saw the likeness of those other two creatures that I had been in my other life times when I had then also flown over their great city; but they also saw that I was not quite the same, but **greatly** different! I had set concern to their minds and hearts, **that**, I could sense, but also 'heard' from their thoughts…

I pulsated the seven rays of the planet Earth's life-light force. I now, after reaching one hundred feet, forty feet above the highest building in Atlantis, leveled off and flew over that city, while they watched in awe, and probably fear! When I knew everyone was aware of me and watching me, I burst into flames of the seven rays, burning myself up, sacrificing myself, hopefully, to reach their recessive all-knowing Divine inner blue-prints that could eventually give them revelation into its symbolic meaning! I had hoped that some, if not most, would take the time to ponder on this, seeing this as an omen having a symbolic, metaphoric, and archetype meaning. I hoped some understood quickly its meaning and shared it with others…but many only turned to fear, or mystery, creating terrifying myths and legends of their interpretations, and missing the true symbolic meaning…

Years went on and the Atlantian Scientists and Geneticists continued experimenting on animals, people and other life forms; even their food, creating adulterated, unnatural foods! People who were fed these foods began to slow down their ascension to the light. This gave the Rulers, Scientists and Geneticists more advantages over them for they used this altered food to gain control of the people with the lesser god's DNA, reducing the people to less mindful concentration, less clear thinking, less intelligence, and less light; making them easier to control, manipulate, and command! This greed and lack of pure Soul from these inverted Atlanteans who were in control, pushed them to seek more opportunities to try even greater experiments and control over life and its creations! They had, over the hundreds of years, succeeded in creating several powerful and larger creatures besides me. The Atlanteans had also collected and experimented with a special kind of large quartz crystal they had found growing deep under-the-sea. They did this because they knew from previous experience, and usage, that those particular crystals could magnify the earth's magnetic-energy field. They knew that quartz crystals vibrate faster that the speed of light, and they had already, in the pass, used them to power machines which they had used with great success. This time the machine they wanted to construct would be much larger than any machine they had yet created on Earth! It would combine the high velocity and magnitude of the powerful styloscope, along with the telescopes they already used to observe the heavens. They had found ways to merge quartz crystals together to create one gigantic crystal! This crystal was twice as tall as the tallest giant and wider than four of them standing side by side! With this giant crystal they combined the telescope and styloscope together, structuring a giant, powerful machine! Using vibrations from the gigantic crystal, along with sonic waves and the sounds the heavenly bodies emitted, they then aimed the powerful telescope at a black hole! They first had sent two metal plates up into space, into a vacuum, via a rocket like invention! They then sent a powerful energy burst from that crystal machine to hit the plates, which then sent forth a powerful burst of energy through the black hole, creating a star-gate! A wormhole, it is sometimes called. When they did that, it created a great disturbance in the cosmos, which also affected not only this world, but also others! The lower, closer dimensions to Earth were blown open, creating a portal from those worlds to Earth! It acted like a great wind that pulled beings forth from their world to yours...Earth! These life forms were very tiny, seeming invisible to the eyes of all on Earth! They hitched a ride on comets, meteors, and debris, because their world was dying! They were microscopic beings that could survive the impact of the meteor and thrive in the water, boiling hot, or freezing cold! Besides these, there was also tiny sea plankton that clung to some of the meteors. And although no one on Earth could see these tiny life forms, they were there, surviving in their new Earth home! Some of the other dimensional beings that were pulled here, came into a world that they did not choose, belong, nor want; while others believed they **had** to come here in hopes of a chance to survive! Those who were pulled into this world were frightened, and in much discomfort! They were invisible to our eyes, as were those from yet another dimension! Those who were sucked from the other dimensions went into some of Earth's plant life, animals, and even into some humans, in order to survive the difference of this planet! This then produced more disharmonies, and impurities; disturbing the delicate balance of Earth and those they went into; disrupting and scattering the earned and much needed and desired peace of your world here! This experiment that the Atlantean Scientists had performed trying to create from Earth a way to inter-dimensional travel back and forth, quickly, to their original home, and to other worlds, had done much more damage to this planet and its inhabitants then it could have done to enhance it or the Atlanteans and their purpose! Their wormhole experiment caused the Earth to wobble, and her ecosystem's delicate balance to mutate, causing the delicate canopy that covered the entire planet to rip! This ripping disturbed the elements, creating turbulences and confusement to, and in all, the elements, and, all species upon her! The Great 'Serpent' in the sky then came down and 'the sun and the stars fell!' The 'sky vomited', sending fire raining down upon the Earth! The Earth then began to regurgitate as well! The gases from within her came up from her belly, and up from the seas and ocean floors! They came up from the volcanoes, spilling their liquid fire and contents down upon all that was in their wake!

Fire from the Earth's core rose up through her mountains, hollowing out the insides, creating caverns on the way, burying all: rocks, animals, trees, and humans alike! The skies emptied their water filled clouds, and the waters that rained forth boiled with acid from the intense heat and chemical makeup of ***the something*** that came from the sky; a comet perhaps, that had been pulled out of orbit and was then falling from space, quickly approaching Earth? The clouds of vaporized water from the ocean of sulfuric acid, sent boiling sulfuric acid raining back down to the Earth; then it vaporized again, lifting again as clouds, to be released repeatedly again and again, back to Earth and above into clouds! Its stink and gases filled the water and the air, carrying on the wind, and on the hot sprays of ocean water! The oceans and all the waters on land soon became a powerful, boiling hot, destructive turbulence in the air and the sea! This was created from the cooler air and water turning from cold to boiling hot, creating circular wind currents which seemed to fight and resist one another; producing, in conflict, strong winds that soon escalated into hurricanes! For the first time Atlantis shook and trembled; and for the second time, she knew real fear…

The islanders attempted to flee by boat while others headed for the mountain tops! The slaves in the villages wanted to return to their families and help them seek safety wherever they could find it, or die with them! The water had risen first before the winds raised it even higher to come crashing down upon the islands and the city! The slaves quickly got into their canoes and began to paddle for shore! Some made it but most were lost in the beginning of a raging sea! The waves began to grow larger with each crashing upon the shore, moving further inland each time! The Islanders ran, scrambling, frantic with panic, not knowing which way to run, or where to run to! Meanwhile, the waves came rising higher, crashing further in! The fire from the sky began falling, increasing as it did! Some of the Atlantians watched as the slaves headed for shore, not stopping them, but wondering if that was what they themselves should do! They saw the waters advancing to their city's shore, coming closer each time; taking with it all that was in its path, carrying it out to sea! The Atlantians then pulled up their invisible shield, plus the tangible metal one over the city to try and protect it and them! In doing so, they had captured a lot of the sea inside the dome! They used special pumps to try and pump the water out and back into the sea! The leaders sent out signals to God and the 'gods' in the heavens, and to any others who were near enough to receive their distress signals, and caring enough to help rescue them! It is then that I asked to go back to Earth to help. I was sent to help save as many of the innocents on Earth that I could! This included not just the humans but also the Atlantian people, as well as all the other life forms! I wanted to save all the children and their parents, the slaves and their families! But I also wanted to save the Holy people; Oracles; Herbalists; Gardeners; Healers; and Scholars; and all the others who deserved saving! But I also wanted to save some of the Scientists; Geneticists; and Rulers, who had been against doing the cruel experimenting! I also wanted, and needed, to save the animals, and those other creatures that could not fly high enough above the fire and water for safety; and those that could not go deep enough down into the Earth, or the ocean to be safe from the fire and the violent elemental destruction! I had a lot of work to do, and to do quickly! The true and Eternal God/s then, sent me my old friends... the Thunderbird and the Dragons! I was so happy to see them! But we had not time for greetings, so we just nodded our heads to one another in pleased acknowledgment, with a smile in our hearts, and flew to rescue as many as we could!

I flew to the city, while they flew to the islands, and to its people and animals! The Dragons communicated to the creatures there, telling them to follow them, leading them to the mountains and caverns they knew about! The Thunderbird herded the people toward the animals in hopes they would know to do as the animals did: run towards shelter in the hills and caves! They did, saving many lives! The Dragons and the Thunderbirds went from island to island doing the same thing; while I attempted to help the dome enclosed Atlanteans! How was I to reach them? With the Creator on my side, I was able to penetrate their invisible protection barrier, but what of their metal barrier? The metal dome was beginning to heat up to temperatures that were going to be too hot for the people and animals inside to survive! I had to get inside to help them to survive! So I concentrated and used the gift of manifesting with my mind, the gifts of the violet ray, and my will, I created an opening in which I could fly through to help those there! Once I had done that, I lowered myself down, feet first, wings held first close to my body. Then when through, I spread them to offer a balanced and gentle landing! Most the people were too frightened, trying to find a way to escape to safety, to give me much attention! That made my task easier! The Atlantians had metal boat-like containers that held ten to twenty people each, and were totally enclosed with two large metal doors, one on each side, which when closed, were water and air tight! They locked in air, and generating and circulated, more oxygen! These vessels also had a thick and protective clear substance like glass, but far stronger, with the strength of the metal they were encased in! A clear glass-like substance surrounded the top part and sides of the metal vessels so the people could see out. These metal vessels could submerge to deep depths beneath the water, and be self-propelled, or manually, from inside being guided by the technology they had installed. Today you would call these metal sub-boats mini submarines.

People were running everywhere, and some of those who saw me, increased their panic, while others seemed to think the other dangers were of a greater concern than me, and continued in their search for their leaders to guide them to safety, or simply ran in desperation to find some escape to safety! I found the metal sub-containers and saw they were supplied with food, and fresh water, blankets and lights that worked on batteries with a crank system attached to each for back up! Families were put together, if time allowed; and if the families were small, another family would share the same vessel. These metal covered sub-boats had been stored below the city, intended for emergency exits for the people's survival; so they were checked on every few days to assure that food and water supplies were fresh and still there. Their city had a lower floor beneath every building, and those floors were like a boat dock that people could lower themselves onto to get inside the subs.

People were running, gathering their personal things, wanting to escape the city, for they felt the heat growing hotter, and they could feel the strength of the water's impact upon the protective barriers! The water hitting the metal dome was boiling hot, heating up both the metal and those inside the dome, rather than cooling it and them, while keeping the heat out! Everyone knew where the escape subs were; and many had already begun to enter them, while others were anxious and panicking to jump ahead, but many trying to calmly wait in line to drop down to the sub-level where the subs were! There were many drop floor-doors, yet at that time, in their desperation, there seemed to be not enough! The rulers had already entered their subs from the floors of their palaces! The Scientists and Geneticists were busy trying to rescue all their work, data, specimens, tools, and any technical gadgets that were not too heavy to carry! The upheaval outside persisted and was greater in its destruction! Gravel began to pellet upon the dome, and all inside began to speed up their search and gathering, thinking they would possibly not have time to return for another load; but, many believing they could if they hurried! The Scientists and Geneticists tried to make a second trip to gather more of their important items, for they each had more room with one large sub per only two Scientists, and one per two Geneticists, so to allow room for the important items they were in charge of taking care of and now…to save! The Priests; and Priestesses; Oracles; Healers; Herbalists; and Scholars; plus all others of importance to the city and its people, also had larger subs that seated them and their families, with extra room for the things of great importance for the community as a whole!

The Priests, Priestesses, and the Oracles hurried to gather up their holy items! The Herbalists and Healers gathered their herbs, medicines, seeds, plants, crystals, and other healing tools! The Scholars gathered their books, strolls, and technical devices, inks and paper and quills! But still they were quickly loosing time! Some lost their lives taking time to gather more! As many people, as time would allow, entered the subs knowing that the waters were rough and beginning to boil! But they also knew they could go very deep beneath the boiling water! They prayed it would be smooth and cool there, and far beyond the turbulence! They hoped and prayed that they would be able to do all they needed to do and save, quickly enough, and then, go deep enough, to be safe! They did not think much pass that to what they would do *after* they sunk down into the sea! The Annunaki-Atlantian technology made these subs not only water-proof and temperature-proof, but also capable of controlling the water pressure of deep sea dives!

The barriers over the city held for a long time. But, there were still many who remained, unable to get to the subs! The protective barriers over the city were beginning to weaken as I searched for a large container, deep enough to hold several people. This was so I could carry them to safety. After the subs had dropped into the roaring seas, the waves seemed to beat even harder as if they were angry that life was trying to escape its fury! The loud noises coming from the Earth were like screams of horror, sorrow, and anger combined! The wind, sea and the sky were splitting open with lightning and thunder lacing the now darken sky, adding to the terror!

The Scientists were sending out strong light beams and high technology, such as crystals; gold; anti-matter; and high pitched sounds; which were beyond the human's hearing sound range, and even beyond theirs! They also tried using other tools of technology to attempt communication with the world which their ancestors came from. They also pleaded help from those ancestors that were stationed on the moon, mars, and other nearby planets!

The Nephilim, and Annunaki Rulers of the city, had entered their flying ships and were leaving the planet! They had stationed these flying ships on top of their highest buildings: their palaces, and encased them inside a large dome that covered the top of a section of their palaces. These were a different kind of air craft then they used on the planet! They were much more like rockets. The dome they were kept in could be pulled completely back to open and allow for the crafts to rise up into the sky, or further into the higher heights of the heavens: Outer space!

I had found several large and strong fishing nets, stored in a smaller building where they kept some of the canoes. I managed to secure them together with my beak. I'd had hundreds of years to perfect that task, and now it was put to good use! I lifted the large net up and motioned to the Thunderbird to join me! She took one end of the net in both her talons, and I took the other end in mine. We flew over to the city, flying over the running people, scooping them up to carry them to higher ground on one of the other islands! The people screamed, terrified of us as we gently as possible, hit their backs or legs with the nets, knocking them into the nets, then carrying them off! It was a difficult task trying to carefully knock them into the net while avoiding objects, plus trying to locate groups of people at a time. And it took far longer than we wanted! The people did not understand that we were trying to save them, not kill them. We flew upwards with them, struggling to avoid the ocean's huge waves and the winds that forced us back and away from the direction we were flying! We managed to fly above the waves and gain equilibrium enough to fly to the top of mountains where I knew there were levels of caverns that had an entry on the side of those mountains large enough for the people to enter and climb down into! We had passed the two Dragons, my former companions from another life time, as they too were carrying people, and other life forms, to caves and hill tops for their safety. After a time, I flew high to view the situation better. I looked to see if any ships from the stars had arrived to help. I saw the Atlantian Rulers: the Kings and their families, departing from the city in their flying crafts. The gravel that rained down upon all of us joined the fire that rained down from the sky! The world was darkening quickly due to the expansive dark clouds that were created from the sulfuric acid being vaporized into dark clouds! All was now black, except for the fires! The heavens seemed to have fallen down upon the Earth, taking with them the trees, and hills and everything on Earth! The gravel seemed to enlarge, turning first to large rocks, then boulders, smashing down upon the fleeing Islanders and Atlantians! The Dragons and Thunderbird tried their best to save all they could, as did I! But the destruction was coming faster and more ferrous! Many were swept into the roaring Seas, while others were smashed by boulders, and the bushes, and trees that were torn from their roots! Others experienced harm or death from debris flying from the villages and hills; also created by the power and fury of the winds and water! The roar of the ocean, flying objects, and the raging fire, was horrifying! Their combined sound was so loud it struck terror in every heart! Those who managed to find safety in caves and caverns below, huddled together, shaking with fear; while those above, screamed and prayed, as they cried, falling down upon the Earth, not knowing how to escape!

Many of the Atantians had managed to escape to safety below the sea, by way of the sub-crafts. Others escaped to the hills and the caves, but many more were killed or loss! The animals tried to run to the caves, and when they saw that we delivered people there, they still ran for the safety of the caves, showing no fear of the people, only determination to also get inside and away from the destruction and horror! The birds tried to fly above the winds and water, but were pushed down into the sea! Some managed to fly to the caves, and further above the winds that threatened to pull them down into the destruction! Those that succeeded survived… It was a day of horror I shall never forget! After collecting as many people, species, and food as I could collect, and deposit in caves, I then took a deep breath and flew again high up over Atlantis, for I could not capture and save anymore species of life! I struggled against the turbulence of the elements! I, Tii--Us, the She-Phoenix, flew high, resisting the elements that fought me; flying over Atlantis and all the elemental anger that raged! I flew up and higher than I had ever flown, flashing all my colors of light towards the heavens to show any would-be rescuers where help was needed; for I too believed help would come, for had not the Creator send me? At last help came! The ships came from amongst the stars and flew down to the opened part of the dome that I had penetrated with my violet ray, and began sending a bluish white beam down, which drew up all those that were still alive outside the caves, and where they could reach them! These people, and other life forms that were still on the Earth surface alive, were flown to space stations above the Earth, between their world and your Earth world! There they would stay until the disturbance ceased and life began to break forth from the planet again. They then would be returned safely back to Earth.

The destruction only lasted a day, but the drift lasted for many years! The land turned to mud, the skies became black-dark, blocking out the sun, moon, and stars; as if the stars, and worlds above, had all fallen from the sky! The Earth was in complete blackness from the clouds drawing up the sulfuric acid that was created by the falling 'fire stones' from the heavens! These were pieces of what appeared to be from a comet, which had gotten caught up in Earth's gravitational pull, and then caught fire as they had entered the Earth's atmosphere! It rained down fire upon the Earth! That larger something that first appeared to be the actual comet or meteor was now quickly approaching impact with Earth! When it did, the clouds in the sky filled with the evaporated sulfuric acid, and became dark; repeatedly releasing the acid rain! Over and over again the acidity water was vaporized into clouds, and then released again! This continued until all waters on the land began to dry up. People inside the caves ate the animals to survive! They were in darkness, and dirty; crawling around; unable to see! On the third day some managed to dig and crawl their way out! The drift left lots of mud; and when it began to dry, sent thick dust into the air! The sky was still dark from ash and dark vapored clouds, which shut out the light coming from the sun in the day, and the moon and stars in the night! No one could tell if it were night time or day time! On that third day, there was a beginning of light breaking through a dark cloud. This is what compelled the people to start digging their way out! There were those who were up higher in the mountains, and did not have to dig, but very carefully and cautiously, crawled to the entrance of the caves! With it being too dark to see, they had to crawl, using their hands to test the areas in front of them so they wouldn't fall into drop offs, nor over the edge when they came upon the side entrance.

The deluge had begun to recede, and the fires had gone out; but the air was thick with the dust from the dried mud, and from the ashes of the erupted volcanoes, and the comet… or *thing*, that came from the volcanoes erupting and the burned up debris! The air smelled of sulfuric acid! Showers of ash and pumice fell, and thunderous sounds and booms sounded with an occasional silence! There had been tremendous vibrations in the air that caused extreme damage! The 'Sea of Ivory', located beyond the 'Pillars of Hercules', in the Great Green Sea, was no more… That grand majestic city of Atlantis, that the Egyptians called: the Sea of Ivory, had completely sunk into the sea… Each day after that, the clouds lessened and the sun's light cast beams of light through the clouds. Its beams spreading more expansively! Life began to return on the planet. Plants began to emerge from the Earth again, and eventually bore fruit and seeds! People began to learn how to survive from the basics given them. They had to begin again primal, learning to rely upon their instincts and the signs of nature and the sky to survive. They had to become communal and learn to respect one another and life, working together for all, not just for their selves. They had to depend upon one another now; and so it was…and the human race began again…

The ones in the subs drifted with the water currents. When they realized their instruments for navigating and controlling the subs were useless in the strong turbulence, and they couldn't count upon them for directions neither, knowing not where to go, nor if there were any place to go to, they then gave up the struggle of control, and allowed the sea to take them wherever… As the waters on the island began to be absorbed by the clouds and the land, it finally receded enough for the subs to drift onto the neighboring Islands. Some of the subs grounded, some perched on the mountains, others on shore. They all received help. Those who had helped them, were not the Atlantian 'gods' ancestors from their home planet, but a friendlier humanoid species that resembled ants; so they called them the Ant People! These Ant People knew of the sacred laws of creation and Soul. They had been living in the Earth for a very long time, and had been watching the Annunaki and mankind's progress for hundreds of years. They were alerted to the upcoming destruction: the purification that to them, was obvious to happen! The Atlantian 'gods' ancestors would not have been able to arrive in time to save them, nor did they want to! So the Ant People prepared to do all they could to help save the human race and hybrids, in hopes that good and good people, would result, having, hopefully, learned the lessons in what had occurred. The Ant People emerged from the underworld, opened the metal sub-canisters, and provided nourishment and clean water to those they rescued. They also shared their caves with those that needed them. They told the entire human race, and hybrids, that if another catastrophe occurred again, and people of Earth proved that they were capable of being compassionate beings; ones that could, and would, co-exist peacefully with other life forms on Earth, showing that they **deserved** to exist, the Ant-People would then **again** help them. These alien species were thought of as Ant-like because they had large heads, shaped a lot like ants on Earth, and had large heads and large almond shaped eyes, solid black, in their sockets. Their bodies were small and thin; their arms long and thin. They were between three and five feet in height; and could speak with their mind! These Ant People telepathically told them they lived in a large city, with lights and many wonders, under the Earth. And one day if mankind proved to them they could all live together in peace, and follow sacred laws, they would take them to their city where they too could know great things and share great peace and plenty! Meanwhile, they said, they would take them to another section of caves where they could live until the Earth replenished herself, bringing forth what they would need to survive. So, the ones from the subs, and the other surviving people, again went into the caves within the Earth to survive. Only this time, there was light and prepared food, plus, all they needed! These surviving people were the Atlantians, but also the tribes of natives that lived there on neighboring islands at that time. And many still do! Other neighboring island tribes in the surrounding areas were those now existing in Peru, North Dakota, Japan, and those close to the Bermuda Islands civilizations, as well as many others. Atlantis, once powerful and beautiful; seeming to float upon the sea, was now reduced to ruins! Once a city with life, tranquility and order...now empty! Its people frantic and afraid, now sharing quarters with those they thought they were better then. All changed within minutes! A culture of superior intelligent people, who, in spite of that, grew increasingly more self-centered; many becoming too full of themselves to survive in harmony with the planet and the other life forms here! That is, until they crossed the line of balance and destruction, bringing an end to their civilization, and, almost an end to this world!

When the day came that the people crawled out from the caves and their sub-ships, they found no trace of the grand city they once lived in or were slave to. The great city of Atlantis had sunk deep into the sea! The city would shine no more; the technology that could have been used for the *good* of **all** was also gone! All the sparkle, all the grander, all swallowed up in the bowels of the raging sea, to sleep there until the time came that it would rise again! There it would sleep until reborn like a Phoenix, offering it another chance, another opportunity; taking from its 'ashes' that which works with the Earth and expanding on it, accelerating, hopefully, into a wiser, more disciplined master! One who will eventually, mastering and learn each ray that governs this world; benefiting all, rather than just the self, rising again on the Atlantic, into a city of brighter light; rising above it; climbing the 'ladder' of the DNA of the Divine; following the example of I, Tii-Us, the Rainbow Phoenix, that flew over Atlantis!

I saw Atlantis sank beneath the Sea. She sank intact, the foundation crumbling beneath her! At first, she went slow, then just as she was about to sank completely beneath the green water, a large wave came up and over her! When the wave sank back into the water's depths, so did Atlantis... I felt a sinking sensation in my solar plexus when I saw her go down, and she was no more... I had known that city all my lives, and so it affected me as a great loss of something that was a part of me! I looked up to a blackened and blood-red-orange sky, for there was destruction still going on! It was as if the Heavens with all their stars and constellations were falling! The sky was spitting out water, earth, wind and fire! All the elements were unleashed and seemed mindless of what they were doing, and where they were going... Destruction continued falling from the sky, burning all beneath it! I then saw what appeared to be a large fire ball heading fast towards the Earth, and... towards me...! What hit me was **not** a meteor! It was **not** a comet! And, it blew me into tiny pieces; scattering pieces of me into every conceivable direction! Each piece of me flared up into flames and burnt to ashes, floating on the wind and in all directions! I had time, in those last few seconds before I was blown apart, to witness what had hit me and the Earth, creating a large cloud which mushroomed upwards and out of sight; spreading as it did so! I had thought I would be spared this life time, and live out the five hundred years on Earth I was told I would start living, returning then every 500 years. But spared I was not... This is how I met my last demise when Atlantis had still existed... Just before the impact that had scattered my body, I had paused in flight, looking up, knowing at that moment I was not going to be saved, and I wondered, why? I also wondered what it was that was about to strike me, bringing about this life time's ending. I had then heard the Eternal one/s say, just before I and the planet were hit, ending mine, and many other live forms lives: *'The end is just the beginning...'*

When I arrived in one of the higher abodes, (this one being **beyond** the Seventh Heaven) with the Supreme First, the Shinning One/s, The True Mother-Father God: the TOTAL ONE, said to me: *'Tü-Us, My chosen one, you have spent your many life's without a mate. Because having a mate involved its own challenges, with a different method of a drawing and repelling force to form a 'dance' of becoming one with me; one which would have taken you in a different direction than the one I have planned for your special purpose, I then allowed you no mate. Those other particular challenges, if you had of had a mate, would have been a distraction for you, slowing down the type of enlightenment I have created for you to arrive at, in the time code-zone I have created within you to arrive at, in your enlightenment and, your becoming. You were becoming what I needed you to become for the moment of the destruction I had to allow to overtake Atlantis and its people. There is a reason and a purpose for **all** that I do and all I create. Tü-US, you have existed far longer than you can even imagine! Even before you were structured into the form you* were created in by the Scientists and Geneticists there in Atlantis, you were! You existed! You existed **before** mankind and before Earth! You first existed in my mind and my Soul. In this place I exist, there is no beginning and no end; therefore it is like a paradox to you who live out your time on a world of lower vibration, thicker density and within linear time. Your mind cannot falcom a place of existence that is also today, yesterday, and tomorrow, all at the same moment. You became what you are today, by way of the denser dimensions, this is true, but you have become who you are because of the future as well as the pass. They influence you and all things, for they exist at the same time! You existed **before** time was even created! You have been with me always, and ever shall be, as are, and will be, **all** my creations! To help my creations to become all that light can create and become, I have encoded memory codes and time-set memory codes of all that is, to be released at times of necessity. These codes contain important 'seed' messages, instructions, and knowledge. You and others, have high knowledge time codes programmed within you; but for most my creation, those codes can be altered to go off earlier or later, according to their Soul's choice. But for you and those I have chosen for a purpose of raising my creation and its Soul up out of stagnation and darkness, I have set codes within that awaken one faster, and guide each to each time code slot that is scheduled to release what is needed to be released to them and to the world/the Earth, so to be released to the many worlds! These codes are released at crucial times when they are needed to remind you, others, and life, of the knowledge I have encoded within them! For you and the chosen ones, codes then are released in the words you and they speak to others. Codes have I also placed in patterns of events, symbols, words, and sightings! They are released in numbers, drawings, writings, poetry, music, dance, and stories; and even in more ways than that! They are released and given in dreams and contemplation, and in formations on and in the Earth, such as mountains, Earth structures, and, the mineral family! These stones, precious, and so called semi-precious, and crystals, hold all *memories of Earth and life! Their colors also carry the vibrations you have learned about. They hold the codes of awakening, as does all above in the stars, cosmos, and in the constellations of the Heavens!"* The Supreme paused for a moment then began again, *"Tii-Us my Phoenix, the Atlanteans intentions were not at first for selfish and heartless doings. They, in their own way, attempted to assist creation in the advancement of a higher level of evolution; but in their haste to accomplish this they lost sight of their Soul and all other Souls, forgetting the higher teachings they were schooled in and grew up in. Not all of them forgot, nor did all of them stray from their memories and Soul and its connection to me. The Nephilim were once close to me, and so acquired great knowledge, but then they tried to be in control of life and creation, so I cut off further knowledge to them. The Atlanteans, and Lemurians were some of my more advanced species, sent here to give more life to this planet. Consciously, most did not know it was I who sent them, but those who were more connected to me, believed and knew I had guided them to come to Earth. I have forgiven the Atlanteans, Nephilim, and the Annunaki for their weakness with temptations and doings, and so should you! They are still children in the universe of becoming, and, they will rise again! They will rise again to perfect themselves and my creation! All is a learning process. They too have I encoded their purpose, meaning, and growth. Remember all this, and always have compassion and patience, as well as love and forgiveness, for all others and life; wrapped with empathy!"* There was another pause in words here, then slowly the Divine Supreme All spoke again to me. *"Tii-Us, My Rainbow Phoenix...You have given birth! You are now a mother of Phoenixes! When you were broken into many pieces, they were then sent to flames to turn to ashes. Those ashes were special...they carried the birth of a baby Phoenix within each. Out of chaos and destruction comes creation from light! Those destructive happenings, of such on Earth, that happen within Atlantis, created combustion powerful enough to transform into an order of new life! From this was it possible for such a powerful being, that you have become, to duplicate herself into newborns of herself that will carry with them all you have learned, experienced, and earned, so to be able to eventually go forth to do my bidding for the bigger plan of creation, on all levels, in all worlds, in all universes! There are now more Phoenixes to mature and learn as you have learned! They then will also be my advocates, assisting me with the balance and continuation of other worlds! Each will, at the proper time, be sent to other worlds as guardians, to work with me for the sake of life on, and within, those worlds! So, Tii-Us, Dear faithful and loyal Guardian, you are at last a mother! Come, greet your children!"* I was amazed and overcome with joy! I was then taken to them. I spend many happy years nursing and teaching them, until it was my time to come back to Earth with my story, and the Supreme All's message..."

Tii-Us, the Rainbow Phoenix, became silent for a few moments after telling this much of her story. She then began to speak again, ending her story and beginning her message, "Humans, I tell you my story so you can know what you once were; where you've been; what you've lost; where you are headed; and the choices you must make, NOW! Don't make the same mistakes of the pass! Be more aware; and discipline your ways, emotions, words and thoughts! For all has a domino effect upon all life! Allow your heart to be fearless in its knowing of right, and the good of truth! And let it be connected to, and for, the Soul, Spirit, body, mind, and, the Divine that lives within you and within all! This is the way to 'climb' the double spiraling helix-ladder, adding another level to that rope to the heavens, and to the purpose of your Creator, the Creator of you! This is the way to your ascension to becoming the likeness, out of the image, that the Supreme Creator/s, your true God, imagined for you, and for you to be!

You may wonder and marvel at how I can be still alive to tell you my story after the huge something from the sky had ended my life. I shall tell you...with that destruction, my purpose was, for that time, fulfilled. After the ball of fire-like object burnt me to ashes, the Eternal Mother-Father had taken me to their higher abode. I was told there what it was that had brought about my destruction...but people of Earth, I must leave it to you, for now, to learn for yourselves what it was. I was told by the Supremes that the time had come, and the time was right, for young Fire-Birds. They would be birthed from my ashes, and rise to also learn of the seven rays. The Eternal One/s said I had to 'burn' in a different fire for this to be. I was told that I had gone through the necessary rays that would help create the baby Fire-Birds/Phoenixes; and rather than burn like in the past, for my need of purification and renewal, I had to burn by the hand of three: God, nature, and man, thus, giving off a different kind of fire! So a fire ball was sent from the heavens, and from man, to bring about the destruction of nature that together, brought about the burning hot of my body to ashes! Those ashes gave rise to other Fire-Birds! My ashes contained the powers of the rays I had gone through, and so the baby Fire-Birds would begin their lives empowered, not needing to go through all I had to go through. Therefore, they would be born aware, awakened, and conscious of truth! I was told I had to burn also so to continue learning of the red-orange ray, only a different red-orange power and the influence of that ray; one that I'd not yet, at the time of that destruction, learned...that one being the one of parenting! The burning in the red-orange from that which torn me to pieces and set me to burning extremely hot, had made me a Mother! The Eternal One/s then told me, because of the sacrifice I had made: by choosing to save the human race, I had earned forgiveness on many levels, of many lifetimes, for my actions proved that even a heart and mind subjected to, and full of pain, sadness, grief, and alone-ness can ***still*** give to others, putting them before itself. *'For this'*, The Eternal One/s said, *'Others of your kind will be given life and purpose! And you, Tü-Us-She, due to this, will be transformed into that which is stronger and closer to my purpose! You will then better be able to serve me and the purpose I have for you and for mankind! It is now I give* *you the name and description: The Rainbow Phoenix!'*

I had flown many times over Atlantis; and I loved the innocents there. I desired to help them, and agreed to continue, throughout all time, helping them to use their intelligence and technology for the **good** of all-life, and so I keep that promise I made to myself and to the one true God...

Yes, I am saying that many of you who walk this planet are the descendants of Atlantis, the Nephilim, and the Annunaki! Some of you are also from other advanced alien races. You have been reborn into the bodies you now inhabit. Like Atlantis then, I assist you now; reminding you of the vows you made to not repeat the same ways that brought about the destruction of you, your city, and the planet and life there, in a time, long ago... You left reminders for your future selves, in case the day might arrive when you might again repeat the same disastrous ways and events that had brought about your destruction, resulting in many of your "deaths'. These reminders of what you and the others of Atlantis did, or were a part of, are to remind you **why** you must **not** repeat history, but learn from it and the **true** meaning of the law of mastery and perfection! When you see me in your dreams, or your memories, or read of me in stories, and legends, know I am listening and watching; and at times, burning your toxic left over residues of negativity, into a Sacred 'Fire' of rebirth and renewal! Any discomfort from this you feel is a sign you are 'burning'! You are 'burning' to 'ashes' that which needs burnt up! You must let them go, and then rest for a while, as the new you emerges as a brighter light, and a more aware Spirit! Many lives were ended back then in Atlantis 's time; and many lives here on Earth still go on to seem to end. But the life essence within them and within you, is them, is you, and was, is, and always will be! That essence is pure, and is **never** destroyed; only changes in its ascension back to perfection! It is what those on Earth refer to as, Love! Love is all there is, and it is eternal! Your struggles and 'stumbles' in life are all a part of creation's learning and becoming. So forgive others and forgive yourselves; and when you ask forgiveness you are also asking the high, original, true Source of All, and your Soul and Spirit, to forgive you and free you of your challengers; free you from the 'playground' that beckons you to always only play, never think and learn, and never leave... Life is meant to be fun, yes, and you are meant to take time to play, but fun can be over-powering additive. Life is addictive, and is meant to be...but, to a degree! It is the discipline of life, emotions, thoughts, play, and fun, that you are to learn, create, and master, while experiencing energy, and emotions! You are to become a master! You are becoming a master of creation and life! For a master is one who can will things into being, but be of a clear mind, with compassionate, and empathy, while also being knowledgeable, pairing it with under-standing and wisdom! To be a master, one must be **wise in all things** one masters; wise in thoughts, actions, emotions, words, and the willing! A master must master the discipline of mind, emotions, words, and thoughts; all things of human! All things of creating! The master is one who has undertaken something and learned from it! Then s/he understands that particular art and how to perfect it. A master has then learned the wisdom of a particular art, and is calm, in control and confident; being mindful and in the present moment of what s/he does, says, and creates.' The Eternal Shinning One/s said all this to me that I have just said to you. It is then The Eternal One gave me my full name. The Eternal One/s said to me, *'My beloved creation, you are approaching being a master of the seven rays and their color wheels (Chakras) of life, along with their influences inside you, and all around you, and all life here on this world. Therefore I now gift you a master's name. You shall this day forth be known as: Zep-Tii-Us, Phoeniasheia-Phoenix-She-ia, The Rainbow Phoenix, that rose over Atlantis! And indeed you were raised from that land many times to be purified, re-born, and then to rise again, renewed into a stronger, wiser creation, with a higher purpose! You have shown compassion for others and for* *those who have harmed you the most. You have willingly returned to Earth and to Atlantis, to save her, the Atlantians, mankind, and other life on Earth, so it could continue on again one day; therefore know you are more than you seem, and more than you know! You are a Shining One! My Phoenix, I gift you these names, for each time you succeeded in mastering a life to be reborn again, you earned a special given name-tone. Names have power in them, vibrating to their particular tones and measures, and then to their song-sound vibrations when spoken. Tii-Us; Tii-Us-She; or Phoenix-She-ia; is suitable to give as your name-sake to others, for you are all that, and so much more! You are also the one word vibration: Phoenix! A vibration those on Earth can handle; but in my hall of records you will be known as all of these, and more! And soon a Rainbow Phoenix of the seven-plus rays you shall be! You are Zep, the first; the first life becoming the creation I call: The Rainbow Phoenix! The creation that burns in the seven lower rays, to ascend further to burn and master the multiple higher rays of the higher worlds! You have become the Fire-Bird known now as, the Phoenix that burns and is consumed by the fire of the rays, yet lives again to return eternal as a Messenger, Guardian, and Divine Deliver of good will! A Rainbow Phoenix you now are, and more than a Rainbow Phoenix you soon shall be...'* Tii-Us, the Rainbow Phoenix, became silent for a few moments after telling this much of her story. She then began to speak again, ending her story and beginning her message to the people....

* *'I have told my story and the real of it that was not understood by those of long ago, those who had experienced me... I carry within my story a message. But I also have given you a direct message for now, and then another for you later, at another time, also from the Eternal Creator of Light and Sound, and all things. But for now know, I, Zep-Tii-Us, Phoenisheia, Phoenix-She-ia, the Rainbow Phoenix-She, that rose over Atlantis long* *ago, time and again, saving them and all mankind; know, instructed by the Creator/s of all life: As with saving and protecting Atlantis then, I was; I did; and am still...'*

The Phoenix, after a short pause, spoke again: *"I must leave you for now, but for a short time. I leave you with words that could be my own, but are from one of your wise men of Earth, HAZRAT INAYAT KHAN, who through many life time's experiences, arrived at a great awareness and wisdom, then wrote of it. As he says, I say:*

> "I have known both good and ill,
> Sin and virtue, justice and injustice;
> I have passed judgment,
> And have judged myself;
> I have gone through death and birth,
> Joy and sorrow, heaven and hell;
> And in the end, I recognized that
> I am part of everything,
> And that everything is part of me..."

The Phoenix slowly looked up, then paused as if listening... She then spoke again...

"I shall again speak to you, children of Earth...

Till then and always...

Pay close attention to your dreams..."

This she said, and spoke no more;
vanishing, unseen, with only the sound
of flapping wings...

"Mankind is not done with.
Challenged by deadly dangers,
He is spurred to unfold Himself
And develop."

---**Robert Jungk**---

"TO BE CONSCIOUS THAT WE ARE PRECEIVING,

IS TO BE CONSCIOUS OF OUR OWN EXISTENCE...

----ARISTOTLE----

2,300 YEARS AGO

The best of a book

Is not the thought which it contains,

But the thought which it suggests;

Just as the charm of music

Dwells not in the tones

But in the echoes of our hearts.

----OLIVER WENDELL HOLMES

WATCH FOR THE OTHER SIX BOOKS OF:

PHOENIXS, THUNDERBIRDS, AND DRAGONS.

- **VOLUME 2:** The Thunderbird's Story

- **VOLUME 3:** The Dragons' Story

- **VOLUME 4: COMING TOGETHER:** The Message
  (All four: The Phoenix, Thunderbird, and the two Dragons, come together to share): THE MESSAGE

- **VOLUMES 5 – 7:** Will be legends of the Phoenixes, Thunderbirds, and Dragons: Created by the Author

---

*TI-US, THE RAINBOW PHOENIX SHALL RETURN AGAIN, ALONG WITH THE THUNDERBIRD AND THE TWO DRAGONS IN THE FOURTH BOOK OF THIS SERIES. THE FOUR OF THEM TOGETHER THEN SHALL SHARE THEIR STORY FUTHER. THEY WILL LEAVE YOU WITH NOT ONLY VALUABLE INFORMATION, BUT ALSO AN IMPORTANT MESSAGE THAT THE ETERNAL ONE/S OF ALL CREATION, HAS ASSIGNED THEM TO DELIVER TO YOU.

ABOUT THE AUTHOR

R. Lowery-Hawk is a poet and artist, as well as an Author and researcher. She is the Author of The Books of "IS", and is currently working on the Second Book of "IS" along with a Sci-Fi fantasy novel called, The Space between the Worlds. She is a student and teacher of ancient spiritual fields and other spiritual modalities. The Author studies herbs and nutritional foods as an alternative means for health and wellbeing. R. Lower-Hawk is of Native American and Belgium ancestry. She is a sensitive, clairvoyant, channel, empath, and Doctor of Divinity., ministering spiritual counseling, performing weddings and funeral services. She is also an intuitive light worker of several modalities for healings and polarity balancing. The Author is also a former T.V. Host of a Ohio cable show. She is also currently one of five members of a women's indigenous hand drumming and singing group: "The Spirits of the Wind". The Author currently lives in Ohio with her family of dogs and cats. She can be reached for seminars; workshops; lectures; spiritual guidance; and other spiritual needs; plus, readings of her books. She is planning on putting the Books of "IS"; this book; and others that follow, on CDs. The Author also plans on creating self-help and how-to CDs, on enlightenment, and ancient spiritual knowledge, along with CD's on meditations, visual guidance, and teachings for one's higher conscience understanding and enlightenment.

R. Lowery-Hawk, the Author, with a six-week old female falcon-hawk that she rescued. The hawk was later released to the place where she was found. Three other hawks, sitting in distant trees, were waiting. They all four flew off together.

**IF YOU WISH TO CONTACT THE AUTHOR:
e-mail her at: rloweryhawk@gmail.com**

☙CREDITS☙

Some of the information used in this book was from Ignatius Donnelly's investigations of ancient cultures, religions and stories, written down in his book entitled: The Destruction of Atlantis.

OTHER INFORMATION CAME FROM MANY YEARS OF VARIOUS READINGS AND LISTENING OF VARIOUS BOOKS, RECORDINGS, AND LECTURES. SOME OF THOSE FINDINGS WERE FROM PETER DAUGHTREY, ZECHARIA SITCHIN, IMMANUEL VELIKOVSKY, AND ERIC VON DANIKEN.

THANK YOU, AND EVERYONE WHO HAS RESEARCHED AND SHARED THEIR WORK AND INTEREST!

Manufactured by Amazon.ca
Bolton, ON